DC SUPER HERO GIRLS

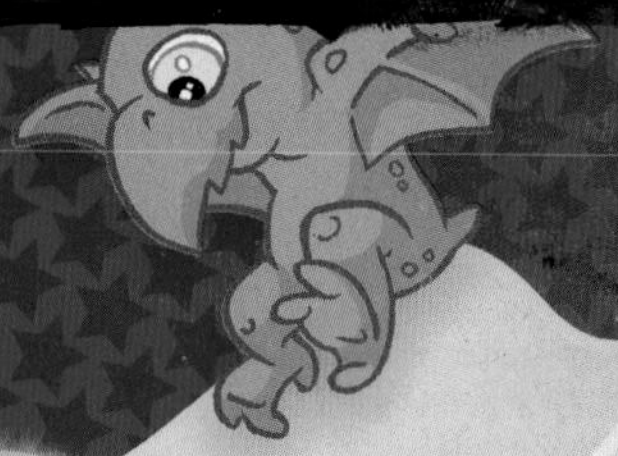

PAST TIMES AT SUPER HERO HIGH

a graphic novel

WRITTEN BY
Shea Fontana

ART BY
Yancey Labat, Agnes Garbowska, and Marcelo DiChiara

ADDITIONAL BREAKDOWNS BY
Carl Potts

COLORS BY
Monica Kubina, Silvana Brys, and Jeremy Lawson

LETTERING BY
Janice Chian

SUPERGIRL BASED ON THE CHARACTER
JERRY SIEGEL AND JOE SHUSTER. BY SPECIAL ARRANGEME

MARIE JAVINS Group Editor
BRITTANY HOLZHERR Associate Editor
STEVE COOK Design Director - Books
AMIE BROCKWAY-METCALF Publication Design

BOB HARRAS Senior VP - Editor-in-Chief, DC Comics
PAT McCALLUM Executive Editor, DC Comics

DIANE NELSON President
DAN DiDIO Publisher
JIM LEE Publisher
GEOFF JOHNS President & Chief Creative Officer
AMIT DESAI Executive VP - Business & Marketing Strategy,
Direct to Consumer & Global Franchise Management
SAM ADES Senior VP & General Manager, Digital Services
BOBBIE CHASE VP & Executive Editor,
Young Reader & Talent Development
MARK CHIARELLO Senior VP - Art, Design & Collected Editions
JOHN CUNNINGHAM Senior VP - Sales & Trade Marketing
ANNE DePIES Senior VP - Business Strategy, Finance & Administration
DON FALLETTI VP - Manufacturing Operations
LAWRENCE GANEM VP - Editorial Administration & Talent Relations
ALISON GILL Senior VP - Manufacturing & Operations
HANK KANALZ Senior VP - Editorial Strategy & Administration
JAY KOGAN VP - Legal Affairs
JACK MAHAN VP - Business Affairs
NICK J. NAPOLITANO VP - Manufacturing Administration
EDDIE SCANNELL VP - Consumer Marketing
COURTNEY SIMMONS Senior VP - Publicity & Communications
JIM (SKI) SOKOLOWSKI VP - Comic Book Specialty Sales
& Trade Marketing
NANCY SPEARS VP - Mass, Book, Digital Sales & Trade Marketing
MICHELE R. WELLS VP - Content Strategy

DC SUPER HERO GIRLS: PAST TIMES AT SUPER HERO HIGH. Published by DC Comics,
2900 W. Alameda Avenue, Burbank, CA 91505. GST # is R125921072. Copyright © 2017 DC Comics. All Rights Reserved.
All characters featured in this issue, the distinctive likenesses thereof and related elements are trademarks of DC Comics.
The stories, characters and incidents mentioned in this publication are entirely fictional. DC Comics does not read or accept
unsolicited submissions of ideas, stories or artwork. This book is manufactured at a facility holding chain-of-custody
certification. This paper is made with sustainably managed North American fiber. For Advertising and Custom Publishing
contact dccomicsadvertising@dccomics.com. For details on DC Comics Ratings, visit dccomics.com/go/ratings.
Printed by Transcontinental Interglobe, Beauceville, QC, Canada. 8/25/17. ISBN: 978-1-4012-7383-5

PEFC Certified
Printed on paper from
sustainably managed
forests and controlled
sources
PEFC/01-31-106   www.pefc.org

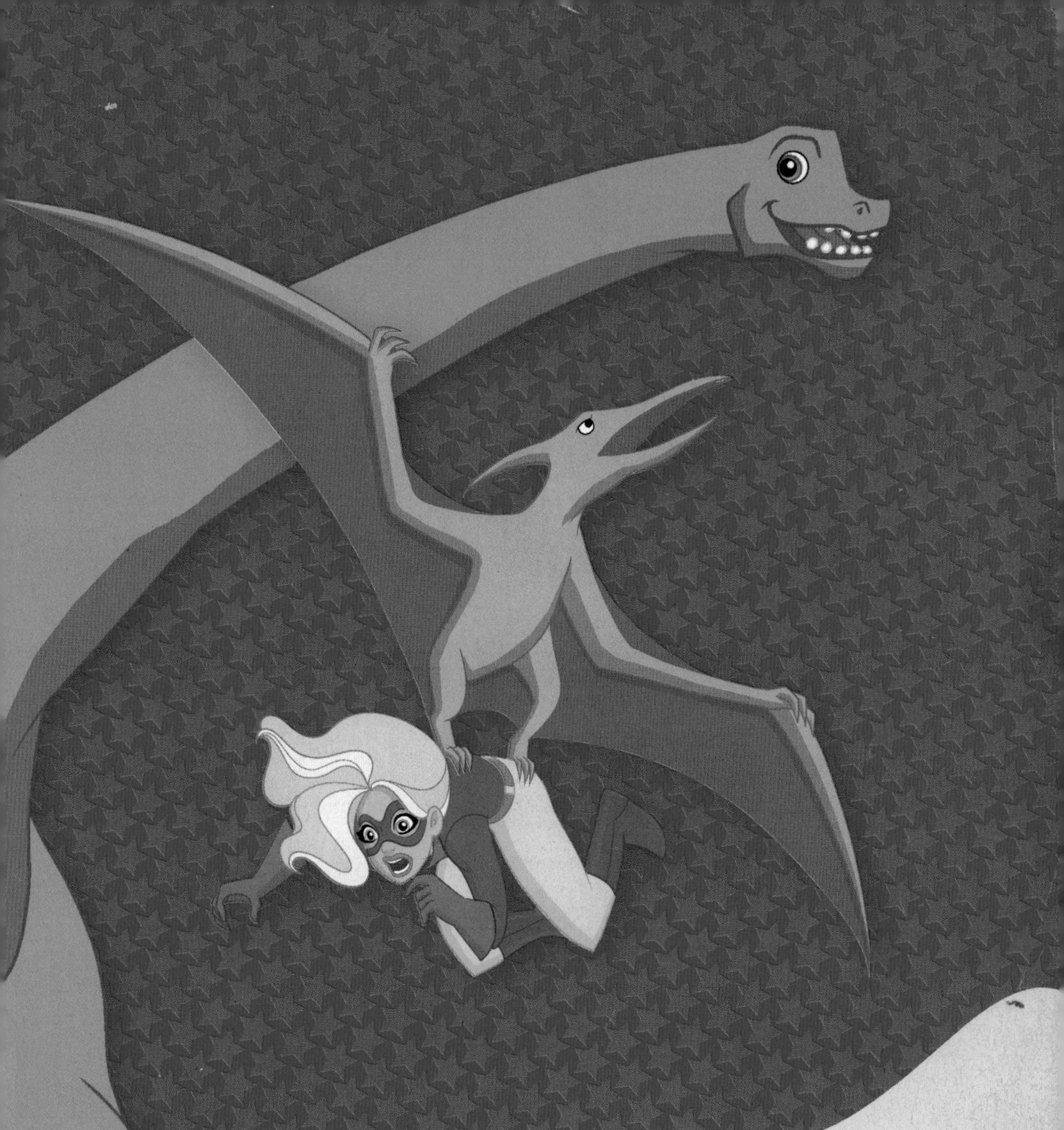

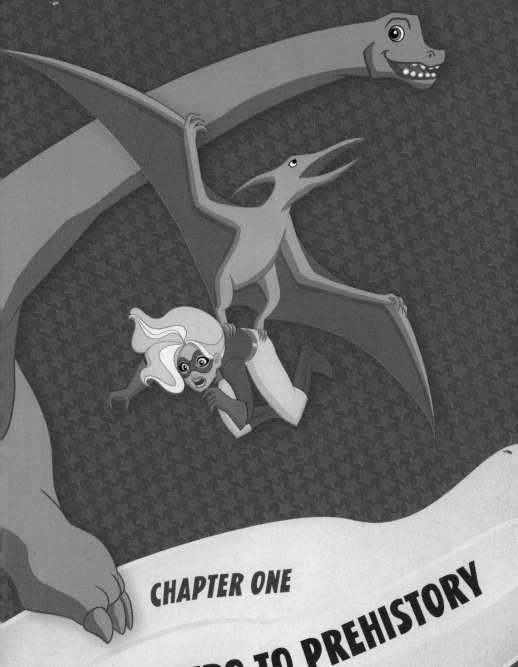

CHAPTER ONE

INTRO TO PREHISTORY

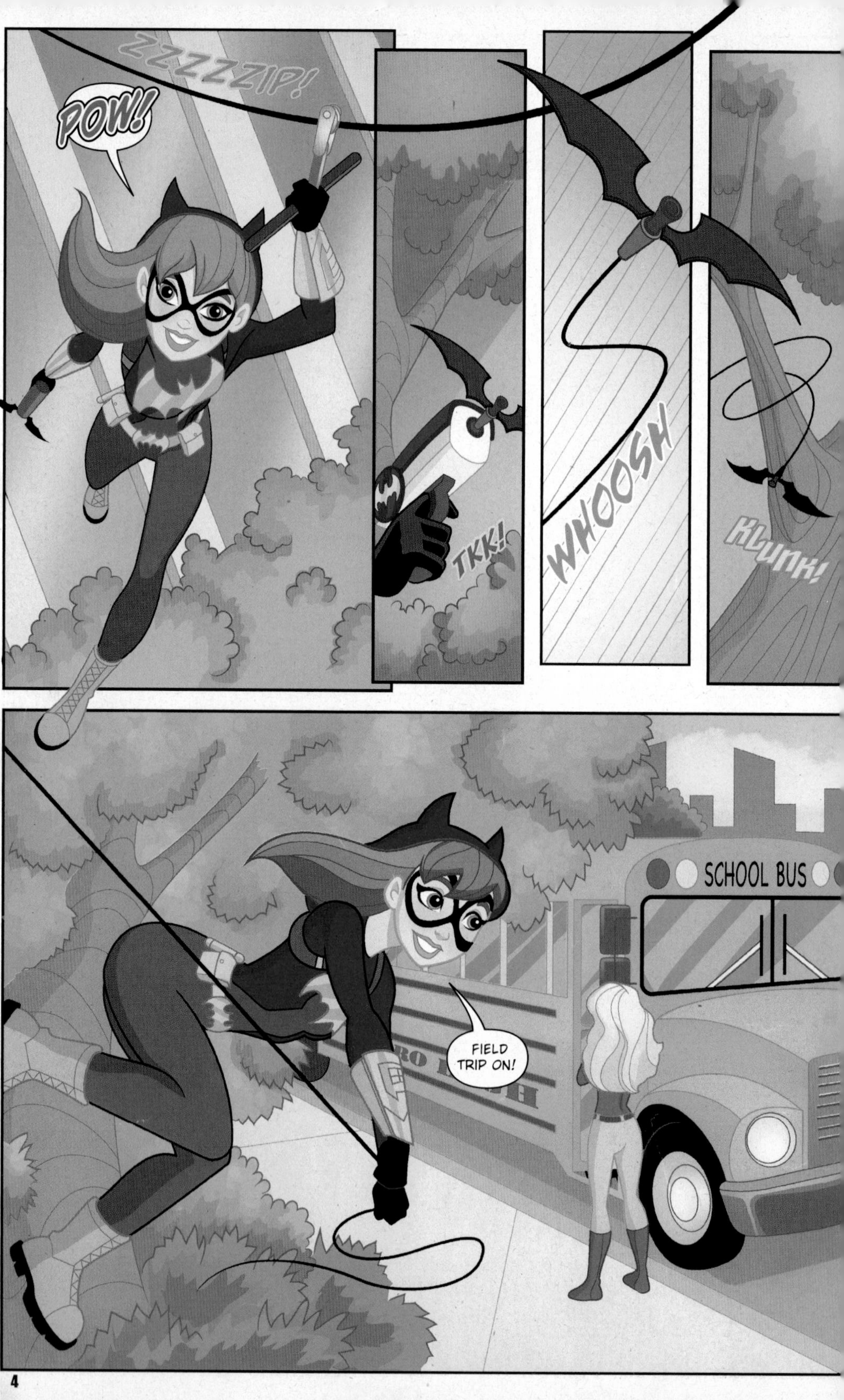
ZZZZZZIP!
POW!
TKK!
WHOOSH
KLUNK!
SCHOOL BUS
FIELD TRIP ON!

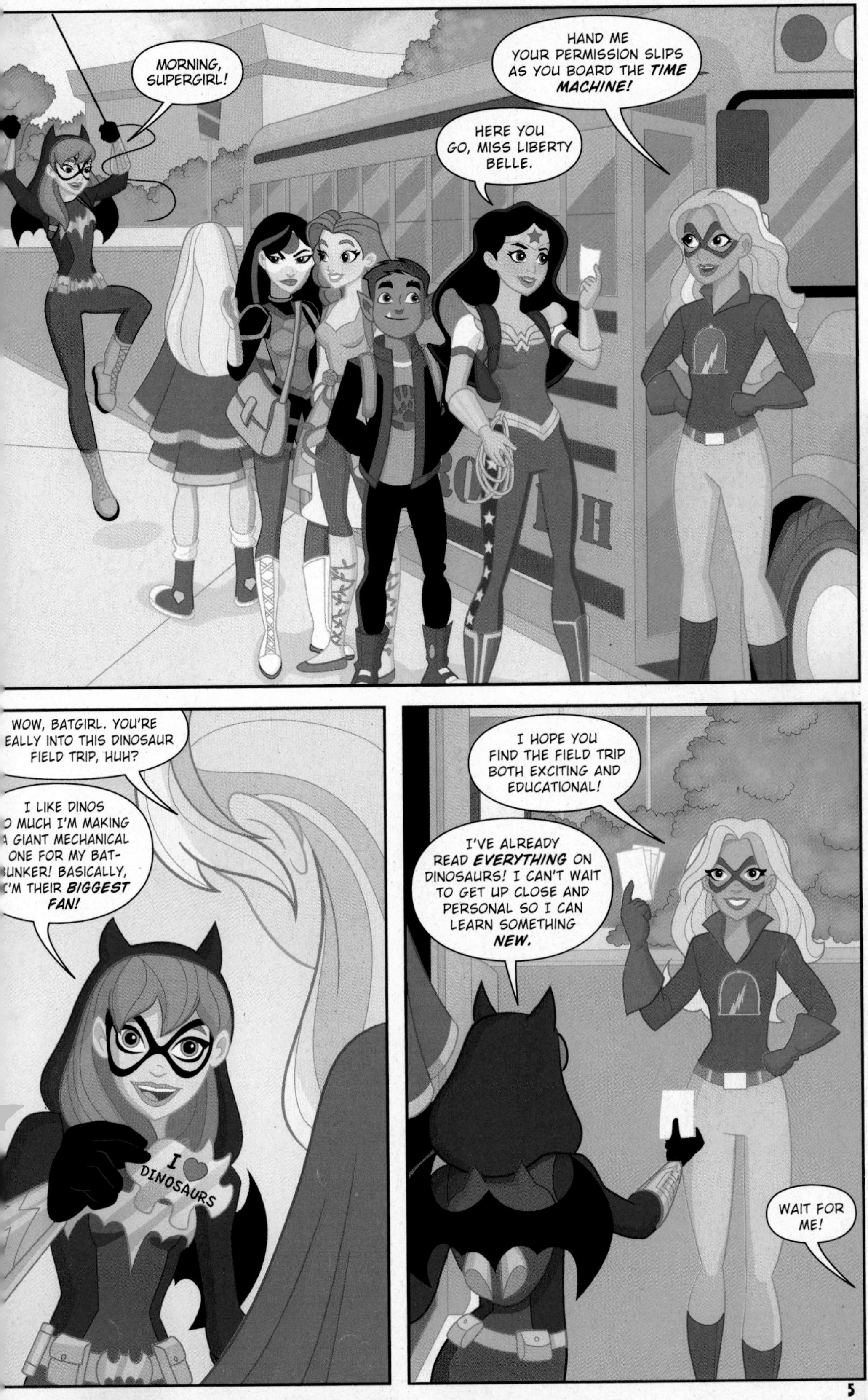
MORNING, SUPERGIRL!
HAND ME YOUR PERMISSION SLIPS AS YOU BOARD THE *TIME MACHINE!*
HERE YOU GO, MISS LIBERTY BELLE.
WOW, BATGIRL. YOU'RE EALLY INTO THIS DINOSAUR FIELD TRIP, HUH?
I LIKE DINOS O MUCH I'M MAKING A GIANT MECHANICAL ONE FOR MY BAT-UNKER! BASICALLY, 'M THEIR *BIGGEST FAN!*
I ♥ DINOSAURS
I HOPE YOU FIND THE FIELD TRIP BOTH EXCITING AND EDUCATIONAL!
I'VE ALREADY READ *EVERYTHING* ON DINOSAURS! I CAN'T WAIT TO GET UP CLOSE AND PERSONAL SO I CAN LEARN SOMETHING *NEW.*
WAIT FOR ME!

HOLD THE BUS!

I grant permission for my student Harley Quinn to attend Miss Liberty Belle's prehistory field trip. Signed, Harley's Mom

UNH!

TRIP!

YIKES!

CRASH!

GOLLY GEE, HARLEY!

OOPSIE-POOPSIES! LET ME GET THOSE FOR YA!

I grant permission for my student Wonder Woman to attend Miss Liberty Belle's prehistory field trip. Signed, Hippolyta

EVERYTHING'S IN ORDER HERE, MISS B!

HEYA, FELLOW FIELDTRIPPERS!

~NGH!~ HARLEY!

YA SAVED THE *FRONT SEAT* FOR ME!

BATS, AREN'T YA JUST BURSTIN' WITH EXCITEMENT TO SEE SOME DINOS?

I CAN'T WAIT!

LET ME KNOW IF YA HAVE ANY QUESTIONS!

NOBODY KNOWS MORE ABOUT DINOS THAN YOURS TRULY, THE NUMBER ONE TOP BANANA OF DINOSAUR FANS--*ME!*

WE'LL SEE ABOUT THAT.

YOU'RE NOT JOINING US ON THE FIELD TRIP, BUMBLEBEE? IT'S SURE TO BE THE *BEE'S KNEES!*

THIS BEE'S TUMMY DISAGREES. JUST THINKING OF TIME TRAVEL MAKES ME MOTION SICK!

I'LL STAY HERE AND DO THE DINOSAUR BOOK REPORT INSTEAD.

THE PAST IS *DANGEROUS.* RULE NUMBER ONE IS NO ONE LEAVES THE BUS. *PERIOD.*

YOU GOTS IT, MAMA! I'M NOT GOIN' ANYWHERES!

NON-INTERFERENCE SHIELD

AS LONG AS WE REMAIN IN THE BUS, WE ARE PROTECTED AGAINST INTERFERING WITH THE PAST AND CHANGING THE FUTURE.

PAST

145,000,000 YEARS

NON-INTERFEREN SHIELD ON

HOLD ON TO YOUR CAPES!

WE'RE GOING JURASSIC!

HAVE A GOOD, ER, *PAST!*

SUPER HERO HIGH

WHOA!

SUPER HERO HIGH

10,000 B.C.

70,000 B.C.

OH MY GOOSE GRASS!

I SPY WITH MY LITTLE EYE SOMETHING THAT IS RED.

SUPERGIRL! YOU'RE NOT SUPPOSED TO USE YOUR X-RAY VISION DURING I SPY!

WHAT ARE YOU DOING, BEAST BOY?

Y'SEE, KATANA, IF YOU HOLD YOUR BREATH THE WHOLE TIME YOU'RE TIME TRAVELIN', IT'S GOOD LUCK.

AW MAN! ~MMF!~

HA! MADE YA BREATHE!

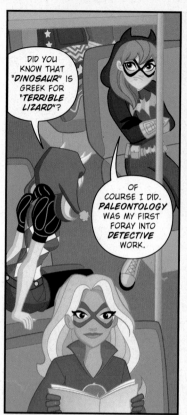

DID YOU KNOW THAT "*DINOSAUR*" IS GREEK FOR "*TERRIBLE LIZARD*"?

OF COURSE I DID. *PALEONTOLOGY* WAS MY FIRST FORAY INTO *DETECTIVE* WORK.

I WAS FOLLOWING IN THE STEPS OF *MARY ANNING*--IF YOU KNOW WHO THAT IS.

MARY ANNING. FOUND THE FIRS--ICHTHYOSAUR, AMONG OTHER MAJOR DISCOVERIES. AND MY PERSONAL HERO!

I BETCHA I KNOW *MORE* ABOUT DINOS THAN YOU!

NO WAY! WHEN WE GET THERE, I'LL *PROVE* THAT I KNOW THE MOST!

YOU BOTH KNOW MORE ABOUT DINOSAURS THAN ME!

THEMYSCIRA ELEMENTARY WASN'T BIG ON *NATURAL HISTORY*.

HOT SOCKS! WE'RE HERE, KIDDOS!

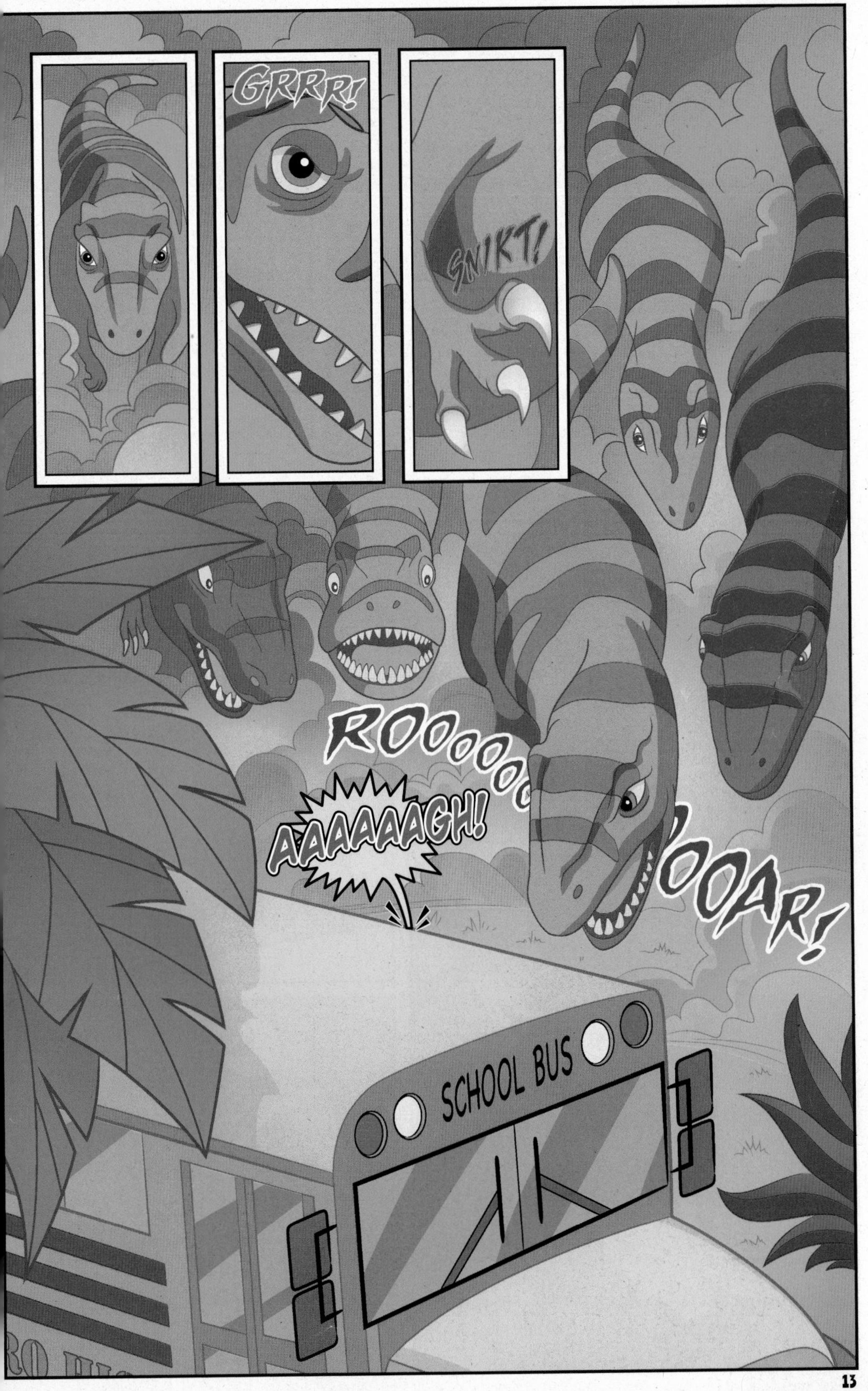
GRRR!
SNIKT!
ROOOOOOOOOOAR!
AAAAAAAGH!
SCHOOL BUS

WHATEVER IT IS, IT HAS BIG, POINTY TEETH AND A HANKERING FOR SUPER HERO SANDWICH!

BEAT IT, YOU BRUTE!

KRRRRK?

THIS NEWFANGLED BUS DOESN'T HANDLE ANYTHING LIKE MY OL' MODEL T. THAT CAR COULD 23 SKIDOO!

I CAN DRIVE! I ACED MY *EVASIVE MANEUVERING* TEST!

HAVE AT IT, DOLL!

WHY DOES BATS GET TO DRIVE? I LIKE DRIVIN'!

EEEEEEE!

SKR

VRRROOOM!

SCHOOL BUS

YEAH! SAVED BY THE BAT!

WOOO!

LUCKILY, DINOSAURS ARE EASY TO ESCAPE BECAUSE THEY HAVE RELATIVELY SMALL BRAINS.

BLINK!

I THINK THE PEANUT BRAIN BEHIND YA WOULD DISAGREE!

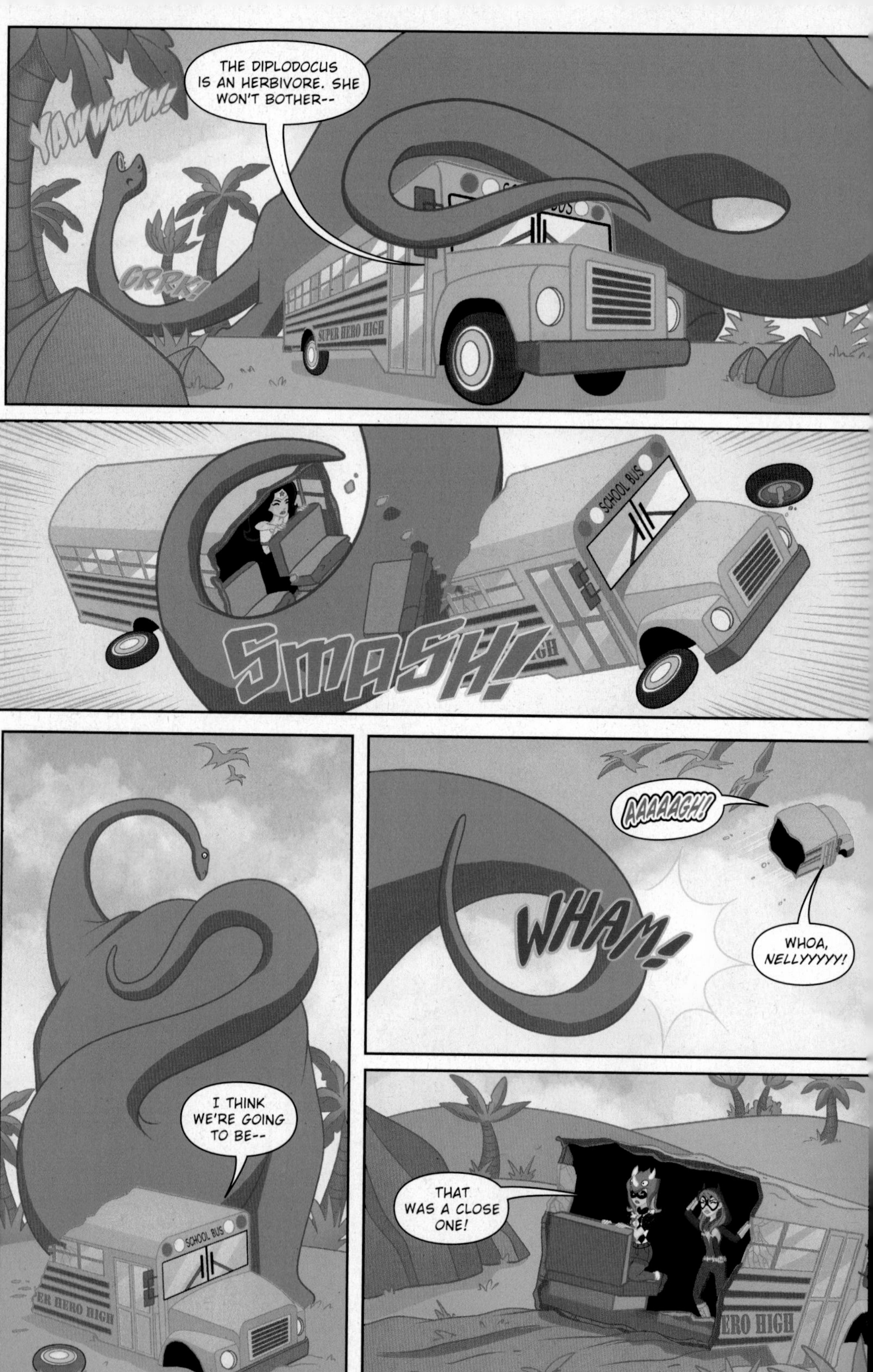
THE DIPLODOCUS IS AN HERBIVORE. SHE WON'T BOTHER--
YAWWWWN!
CRRK!
SUPER HERO HIGH
SCHOOL BUS
SMASH!
I THINK WE'RE GOING TO BE--
SCHOOL BUS
ER HERO HIGH
AAAAAGH!
WHAM!
WHOA, NELLYYYYY!
THAT WAS A CLOSE ONE!
ERO HIGH

EVERYBODY STAY INSIDE!

MISS BELLE SAID AS LONG AS WE'RE IN THE BUS, WE CAN'T DO ANYTHING TO MESS UP THE FUTURE.

TIME TRAVEL RULES

1. STAY INSIDE OF THE BUS.
2. TAKE NOTHING, LEAVE NOTHING.
3. ALERT DRIVER IF YOU SUSPECT ALTERATION OF TIME.

I KNEW YOU SHOULD NEVER TRUST AN HERBIVORE! NASTY PLANT-EATER!

WHOA, IVY! DON'T GO STEREOTYPIN' US VEGETARIANS. WE DIDN'T ALL THROW MISS BELLE, BATGIRL, AND HARLEY ACROSS THE JUNGLE!

THE FRONT OF THE BUS COULDN'T HAVE GONE VERY FAR.

KATANA'S RIGHT. THEY'LL BE HERE SOON!

SOUNDS LIKE I GOTS TIME FOR A CAT NAP!

MISS BELLE MUST'VE BEEN STUCK IN THE BACK OF THE BUS WHEN WE WENT FLYING. SHE'LL BE HERE FOR US ASAP!

DOUBTFUL!

WHY DO YOU HAVE TO ARGUE WITH EVERYTHING I SAY?

I DON'T *HAFTA.* I REALLY THOUGHT IT WAS *DOUBTFUL* SINCE MISS BELLE IS CURRENTLY BEING TEACHER-NAPPED BY A PTERODACTYL.

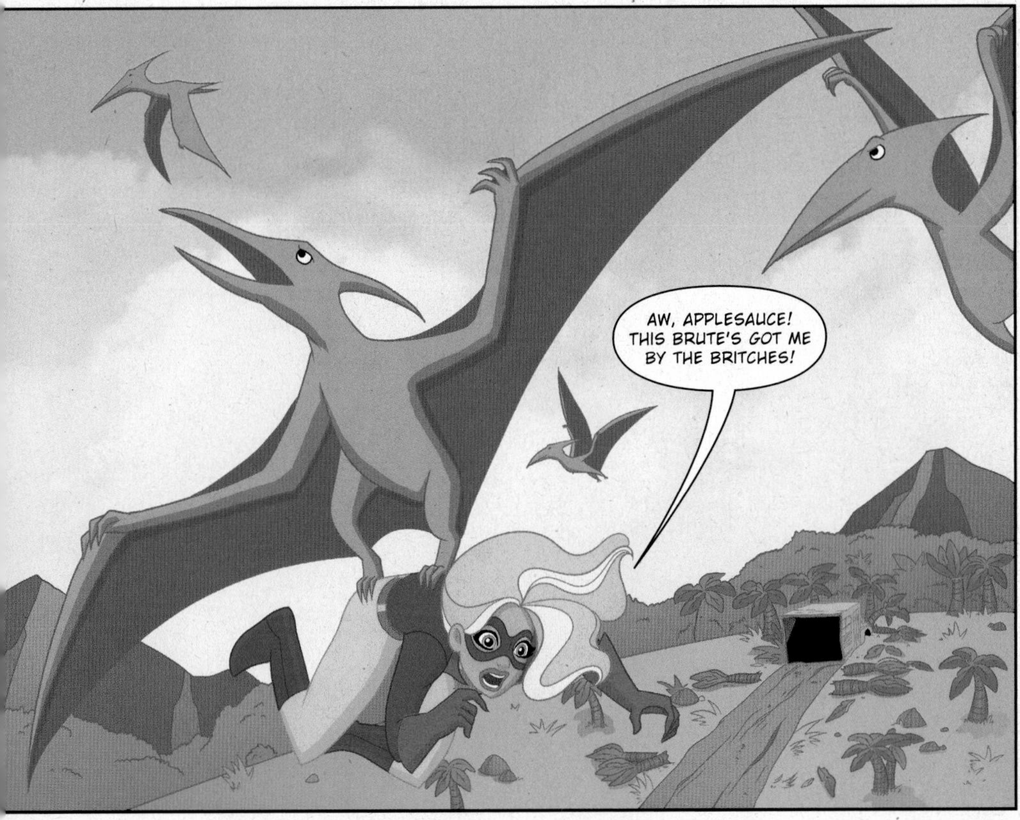
AW, APPLESAUCE! THIS BRUTE'S GOT ME BY THE BRITCHES!

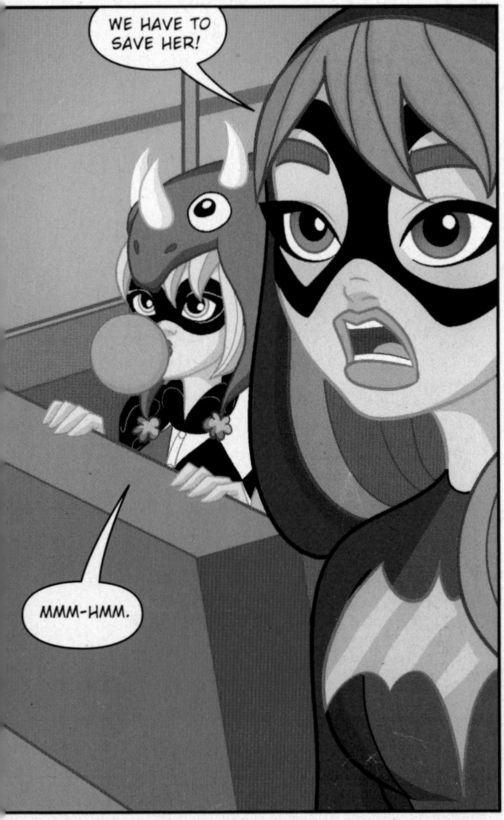
WE HAVE TO SAVE HER!
MMM-HMM.

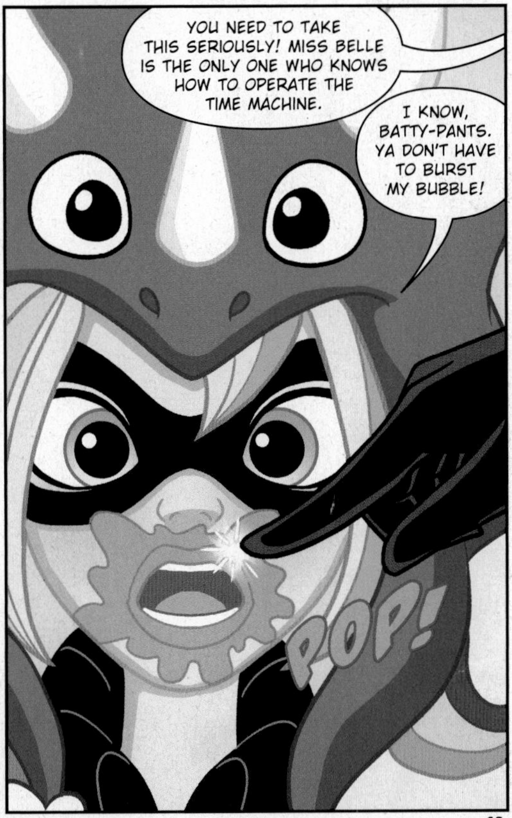
YOU NEED TO TAKE THIS SERIOUSLY! MISS BELLE IS THE ONLY ONE WHO KNOWS HOW TO OPERATE THE TIME MACHINE.
I KNOW, BATTY-PANTS. YA DON'T HAVE TO BURST MY BUBBLE!
POP!

MISS BELLE BETTER GET HERE ON THE DOUBLE CUZ I AM STARVIN'!

SNIFF! SNIFF!

ALLS I HAD FOR BREAKFAST WAS THREE WAFFLES, SIX BANANAS, FOUR BOWLS OF QUACKOPUFFS, TWO SLICES OF LEFTOVER PIZZA...

GROWLL!

SLURP!

...AND HALF OF AN ENGLISH MUFFIN-- I'M WATCHIN' MY FIGURE.

BEAST BOY ISN'T THE ONLY ONE HUNGRY FOR LUNCH. STAND ASIDE, LIZARD-LIPS!

GRRRR!

EXIT

EMERGENCY EXIT ONLY

I MEANT "LIZARD-LIPS" AS A COMPLIMENT!

WE HAVE TO BREAK THE RULES BEFORE THAT DINO BREAKS US!

LET'S GET OUT OF HERE!

THIS QUALIFIES AS AN EMERGENCY!

HANG ON!

I GOT YOU, BEAST BOY!

THIS IS THE CLOSEST I'VE EVER BEEN TO A GIRL HOLDIN' MY HAND!

NGN!

CHOMP!

CHAPTER TWO

THE DINO EGG EFFECT

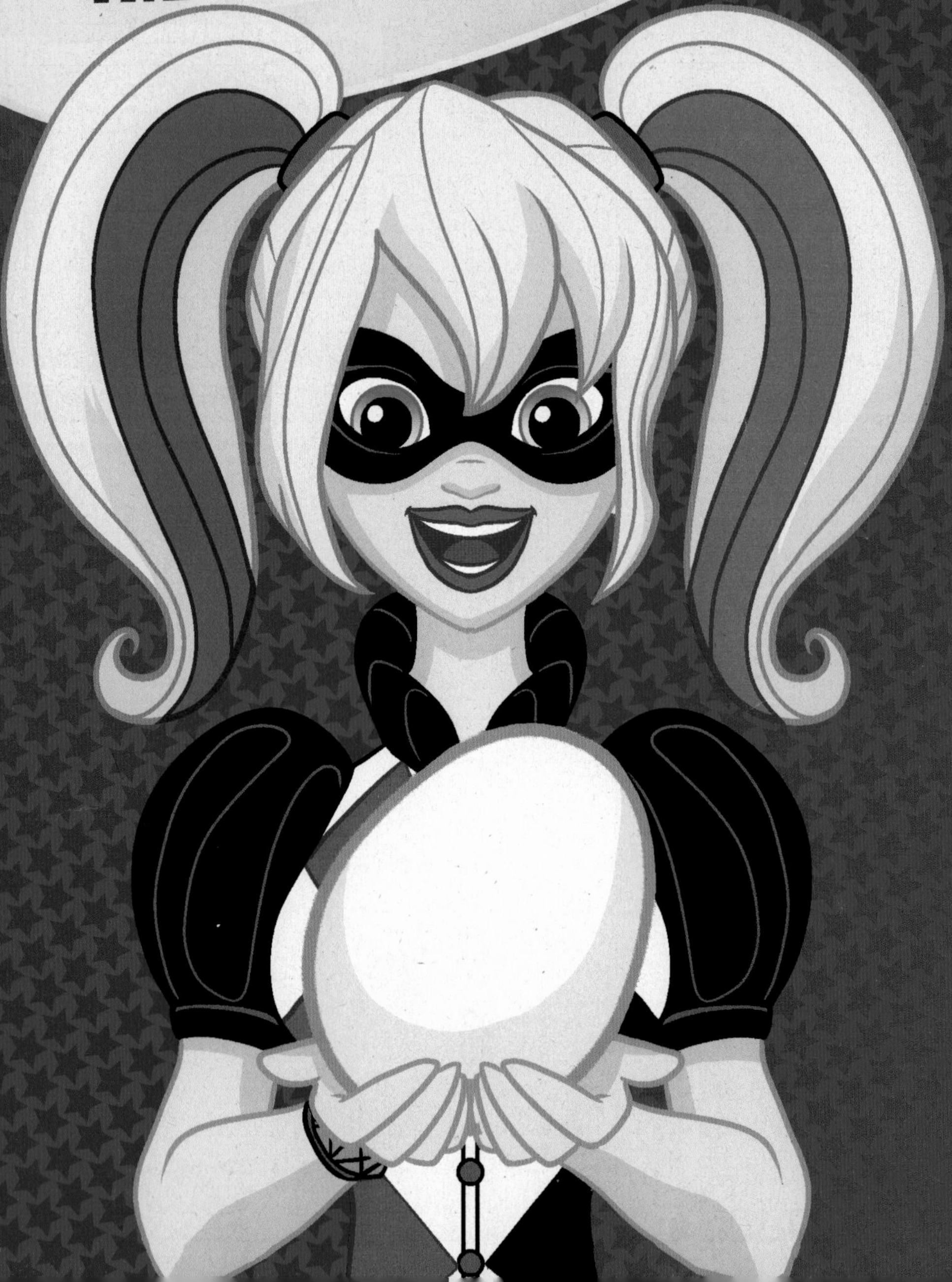

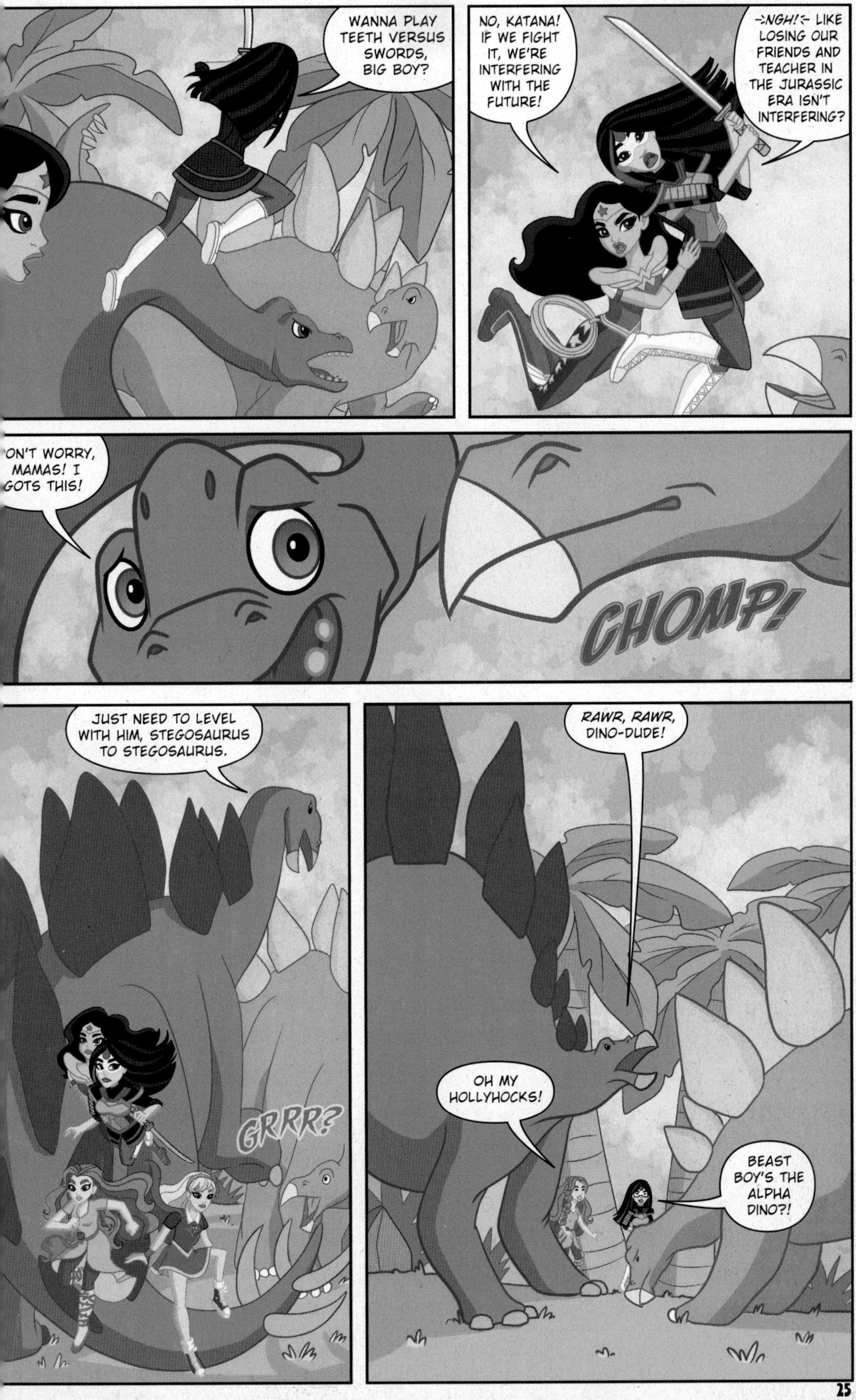
WANNA PLAY TEETH VERSUS SWORDS, BIG BOY?
NO, KATANA! IF WE FIGHT IT, WE'RE INTERFERING WITH THE FUTURE!
-NGH!- LIKE LOSING OUR FRIENDS AND TEACHER IN THE JURASSIC ERA ISN'T INTERFERING?
ON'T WORRY, MAMAS! I GOTS THIS!
CHOMP!
JUST NEED TO LEVEL WITH HIM, STEGOSAURUS TO STEGOSAURUS.
GRRR?
RAWR, RAWR, DINO-DUDE!
OH MY HOLLYHOCKS!
BEAST BOY'S THE ALPHA DINO?!

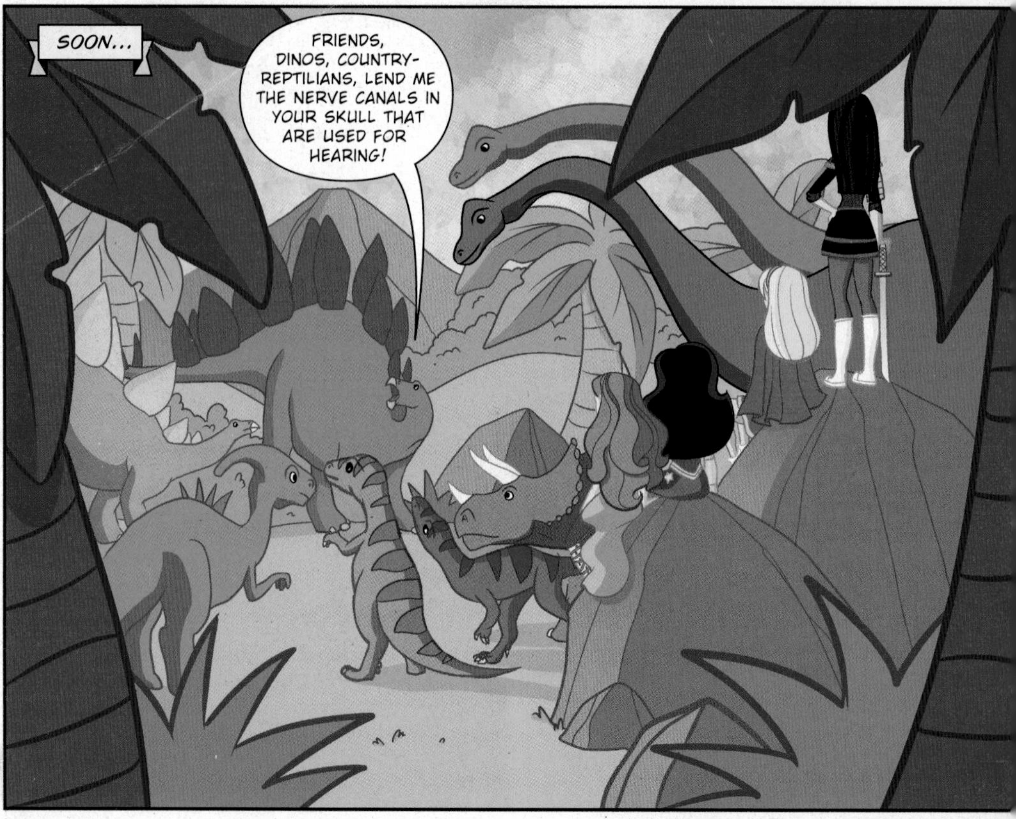
SOON...
FRIENDS, DINOS, COUNTRY-REPTILIANS, LEND ME THE NERVE CANALS IN YOUR SKULL THAT ARE USED FOR HEARING!

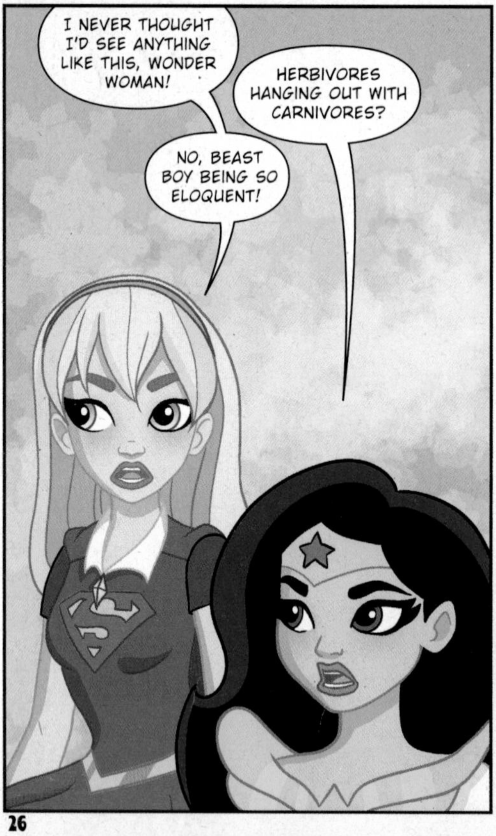
I NEVER THOUGHT I'D SEE ANYTHING LIKE THIS, WONDER WOMAN!
HERBIVORES HANGING OUT WITH CARNIVORES?
NO, BEAST BOY BEING SO ELOQUENT!

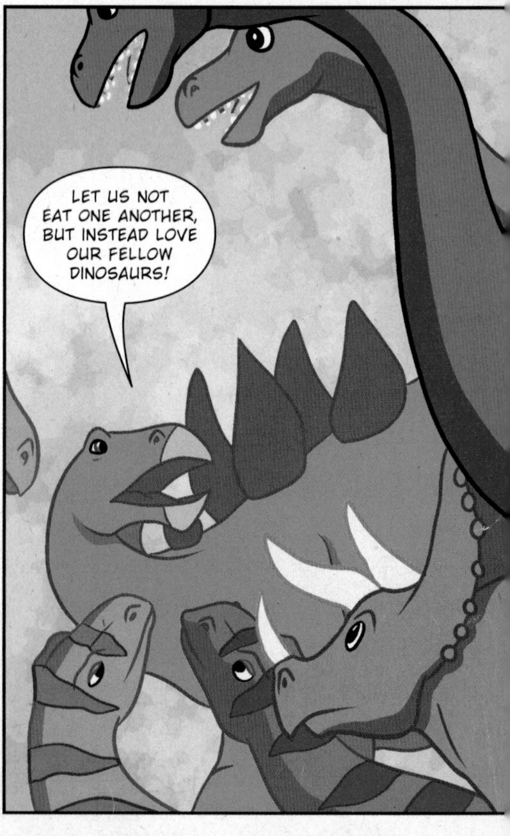
LET US NOT EAT ONE ANOTHER, BUT INSTEAD LOVE OUR FELLOW DINOSAURS!

OF COURSE YA CAN, BATS. YOU KNOW HOW TO DO *EVERYTHING.*

THE DAMAGE IS MOSTLY COSMETIC. I CAN GET THIS BABY UP AND RUNNING IN A FLASH!

THEN, WE'LL BE ON OUR WAY TO RESCUE MISS LIBERTY BELLE FROM THAT PTERODACTYL IN NO TIME!

ANYTHING I CAN DO TO HELP GET THIS SHOW ON THE ROAD?

NOPE. I HAVE IT UNDER CONTROL, HARLEY.

CLANK!

CLINK!

CLANK!

-;SIGH.;-

POW! TIME MACHINE ON!

VRrrOOMM!

VVVVVRMMM...

LUCKILY, I KEEP A PAIR OF BINOCULARS IN MY BACKPACK! PERFECT FOR SPOTTIN' LOST TEACHERS!

I FOUND A CLUE!

OF COURSE YA DID.

HELP!

MISS BELLE!

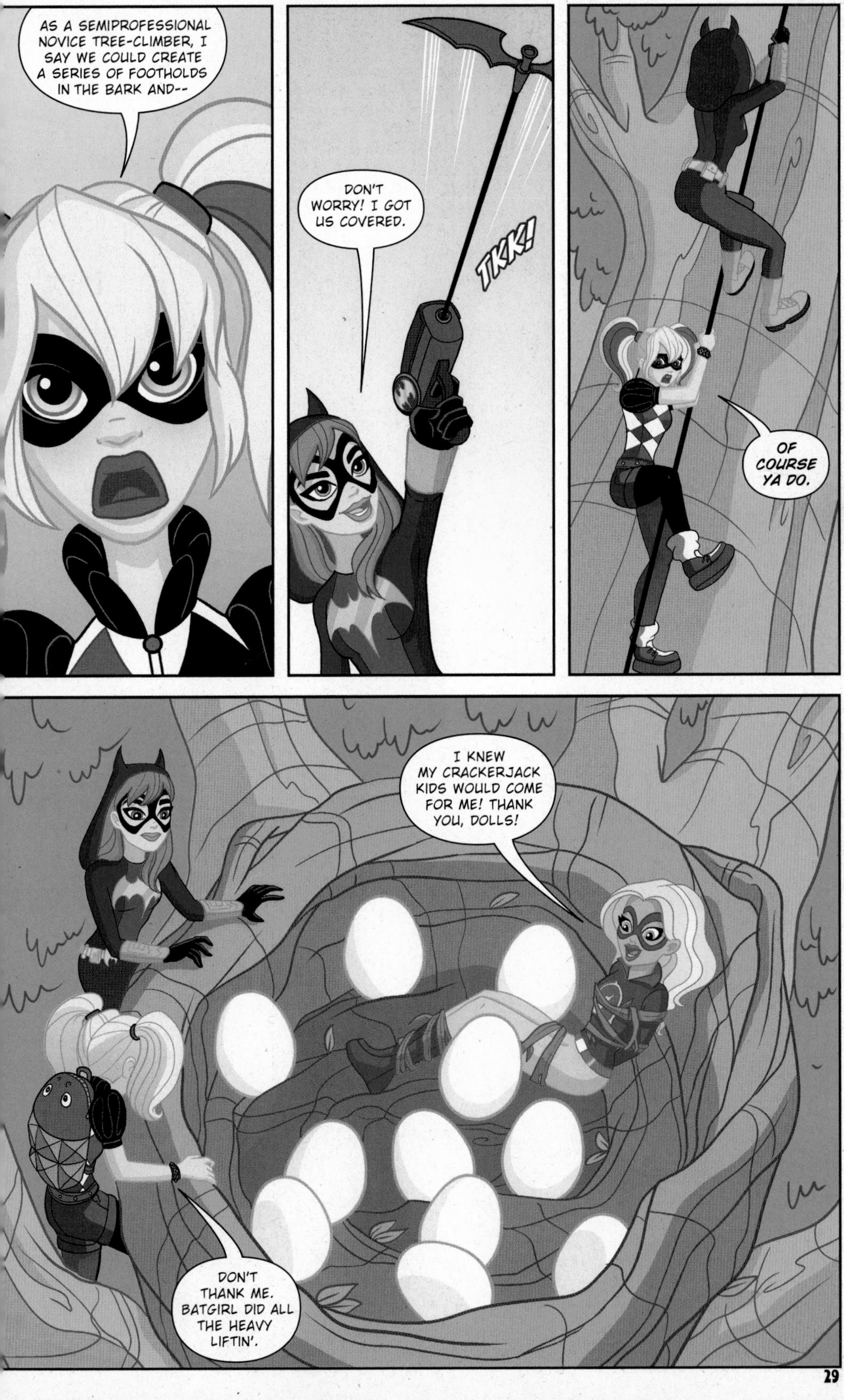
AS A SEMIPROFESSIONAL NOVICE TREE-CLIMBER, I SAY WE COULD CREATE A SERIES OF FOOTHOLDS IN THE BARK AND--
DON'T WORRY! I GOT US COVERED.
TKK!
OF COURSE YA DO.
I KNEW MY CRACKERJACK KIDS WOULD COME FOR ME! THANK YOU, DOLLS!
DON'T THANK ME. BATGIRL DID ALL THE HEAVY LIFTIN'.

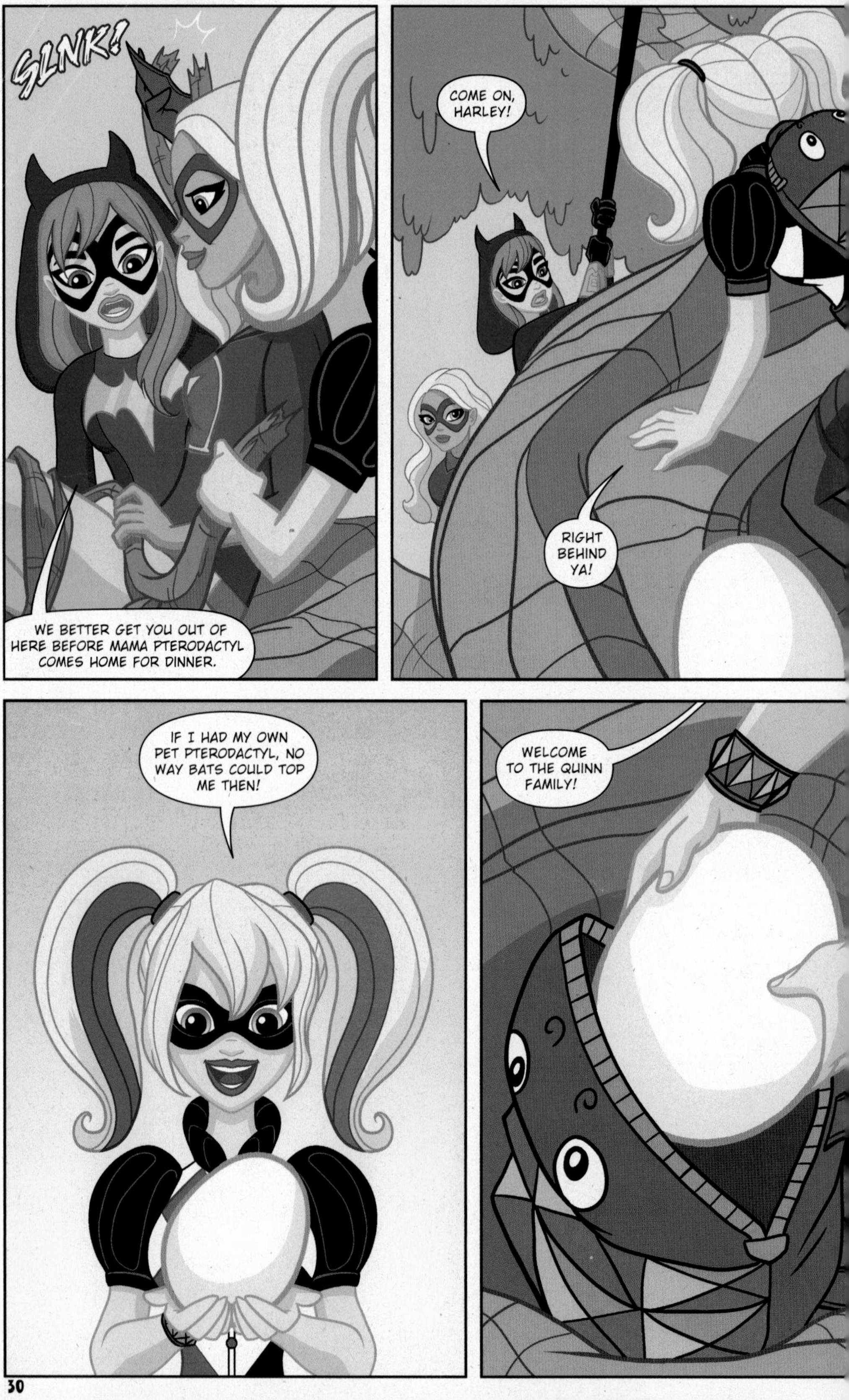
SLNK!
WE BETTER GET YOU OUT OF HERE BEFORE MAMA PTERODACTYL COMES HOME FOR DINNER.
COME ON, HARLEY!
RIGHT BEHIND YA!
IF I HAD MY OWN PET PTERODACTYL, NO WAY BATS COULD TOP ME THEN!
WELCOME TO THE QUINN FAMILY!

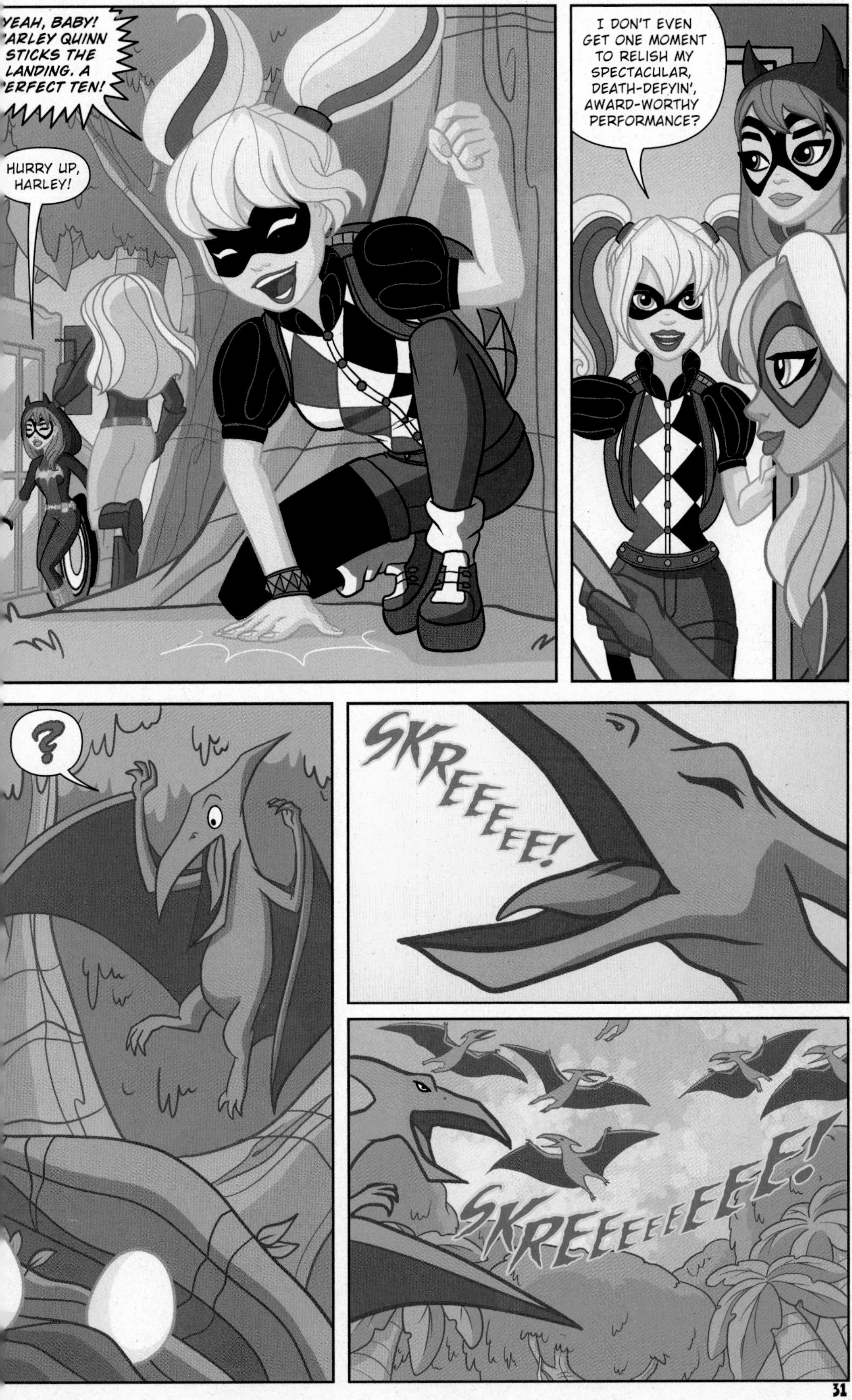
YEAH, BABY! HARLEY QUINN STICKS THE LANDING. A PERFECT TEN!
HURRY UP, HARLEY!
I DON'T EVEN GET ONE MOMENT TO RELISH MY SPECTACULAR, DEATH-DEFYIN', AWARD-WORTHY PERFORMANCE?
?
SKREEEEEE!
SKREEEEEEEEEE!

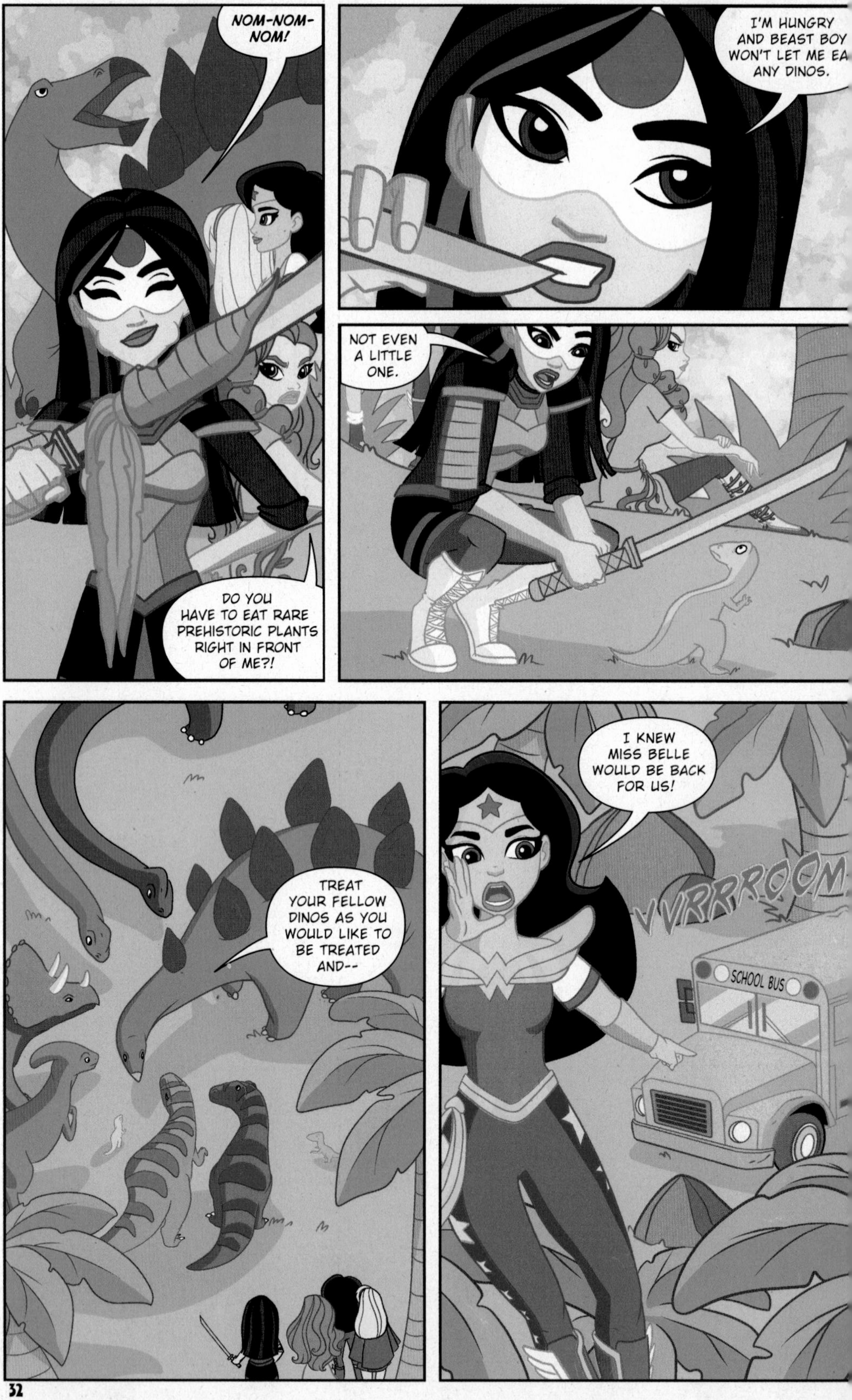
NOM-NOM-NOM!
I'M HUNGRY AND BEAST BOY WON'T LET ME EA ANY DINOS.
DO YOU HAVE TO EAT RARE PREHISTORIC PLANTS RIGHT IN FRONT OF ME?!
NOT EVEN A LITTLE ONE.
TREAT YOUR FELLOW DINOS AS YOU WOULD LIKE TO BE TREATED AND--
I KNEW MISS BELLE WOULD BE BACK FOR US!
VVRRROOM
SCHOOL BUS

EVERYBODY INTO THE TIME MACHINE!

SKKKKKK!

AW, MAN! I WAS GETTIN' USED TO BEING THEIR POWERFUL BUT BENEVOLENT LEADER!

THANK HERA! I DIDN'T WANT TO LIVE IN A WORLD WITHOUT MODERN PLUMBING.

OR TEXT MESSAGES!

EXCUSE ME. IF YOU WOULDN'T MIND SQUEEZING IN A LITTLE?

PUBLIC TRANSPORTATION CAN BE SO CROWDED.

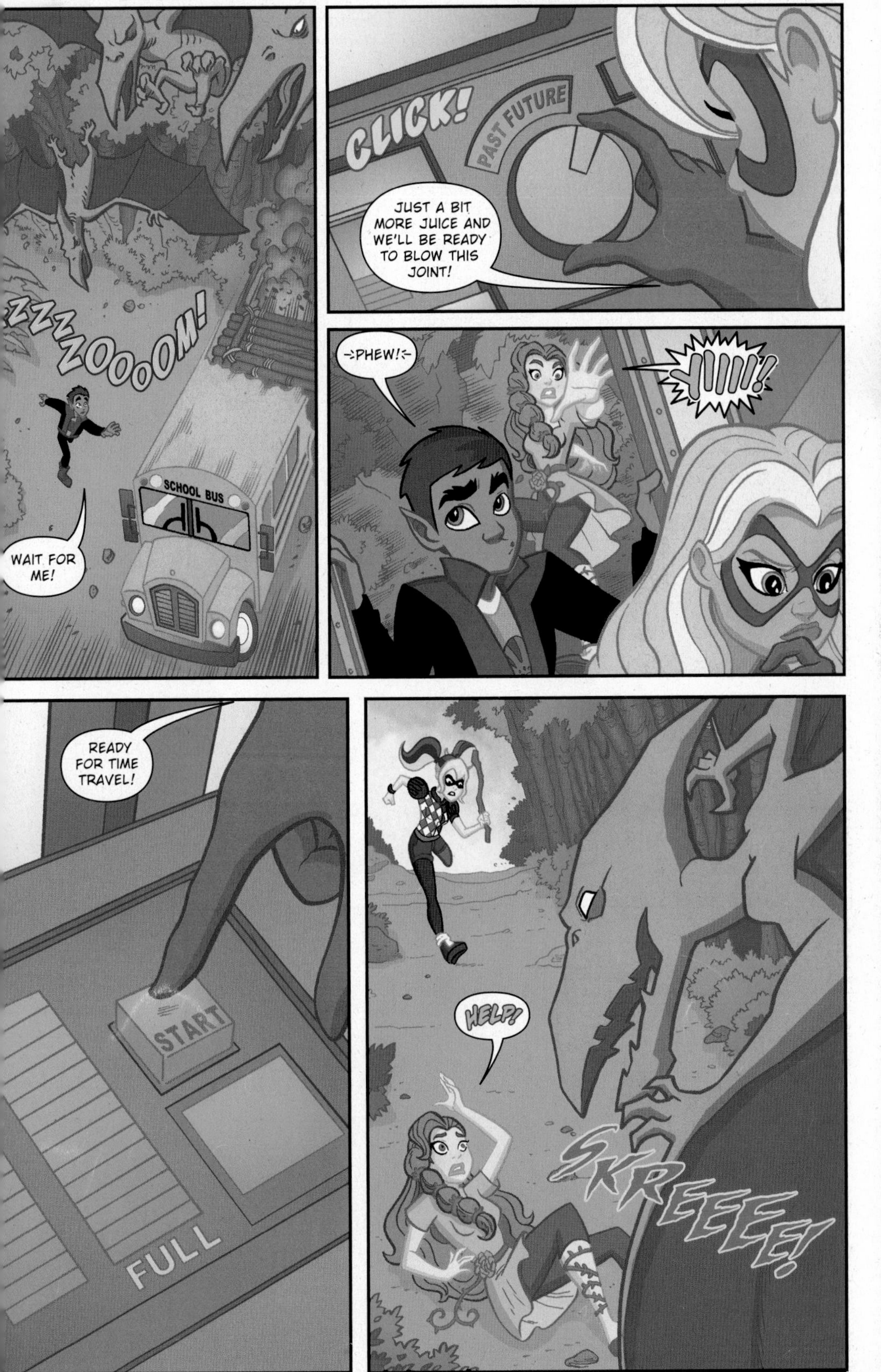
ZZZZOOOOOM!
WAIT FOR ME!
CLICK!
PAST FUTURE
JUST A BIT MORE JUICE AND WE'LL BE READY TO BLOW THIS JOINT!
SCHOOL BUS
-PHEW!-
YIIII!
READY FOR TIME TRAVEL!
START
FULL
HELP!
SKREEEEE!

STAY AWAY FROM MY IVY!

SKRF

THANKS!

WE'RE NOT OUTTA DODGE YET. MISTAH CRANKY BEAK HAS PALS IN HIGH PLACES!

FANCY SEEIN' YOU GALS HERE!

NO HERO LEFT BEHIND.

ESPECIALLY NOT MILLIONS OF YEARS BEHIND!

ANYBODY TAKE COACH WILDCAT'S DINOSAUR COMBAT ELECTIVE?

NEGATIVE.

I DID BASKET WEAVING INSTEAD.

NUH-UH.

THEN WE JUST WING IT!

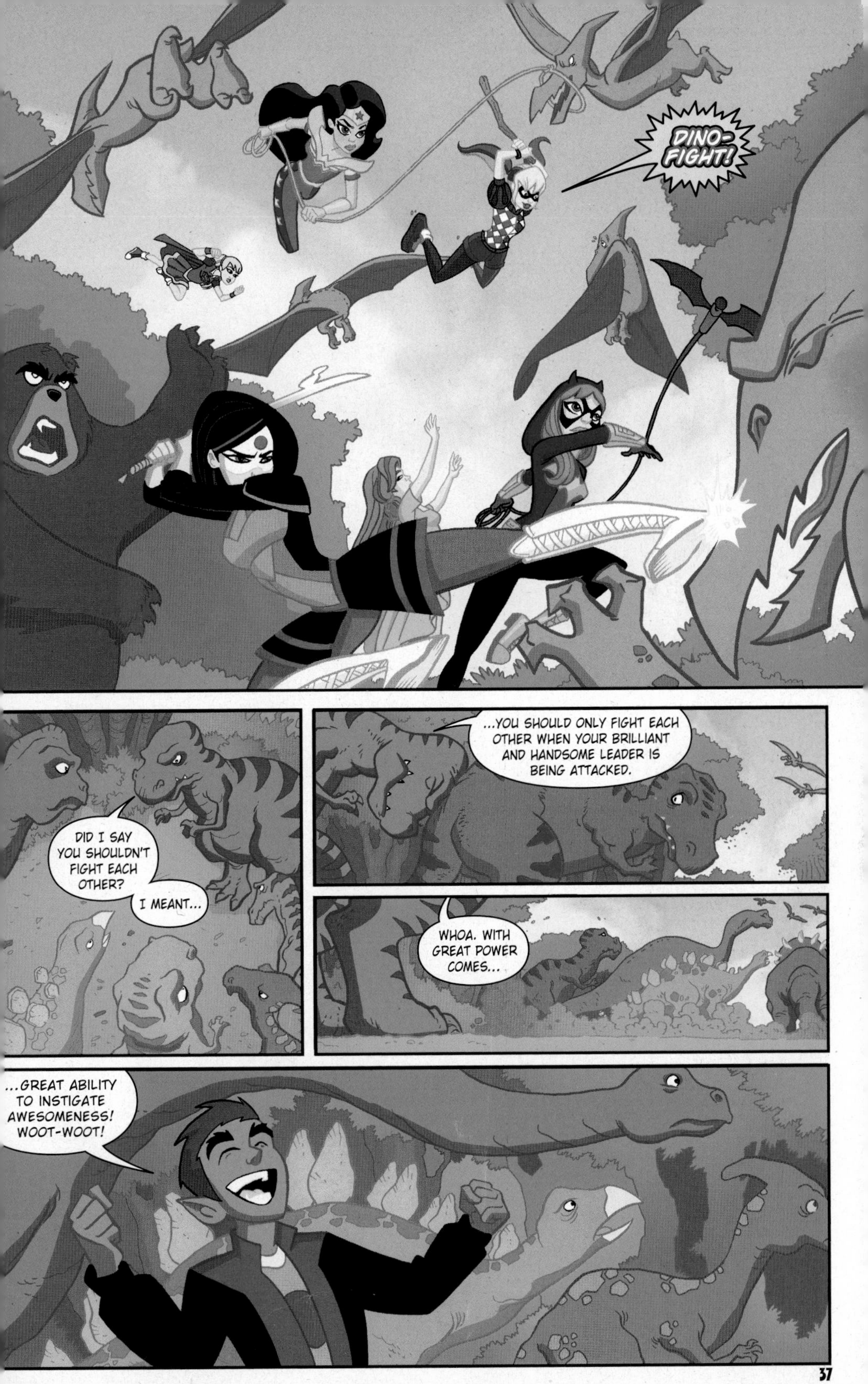
DINO-FIGHT!
DID I SAY YOU SHOULDN'T FIGHT EACH OTHER?
I MEANT...
...YOU SHOULD ONLY FIGHT EACH OTHER WHEN YOUR BRILLIANT AND HANDSOME LEADER IS BEING ATTACKED.
WHOA. WITH GREAT POWER COMES...
...GREAT ABILITY TO INSTIGATE AWESOMENESS! WOOT-WOOT!

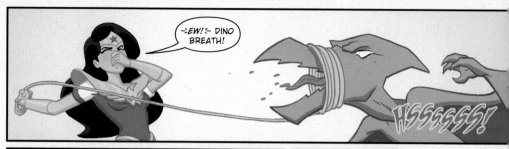

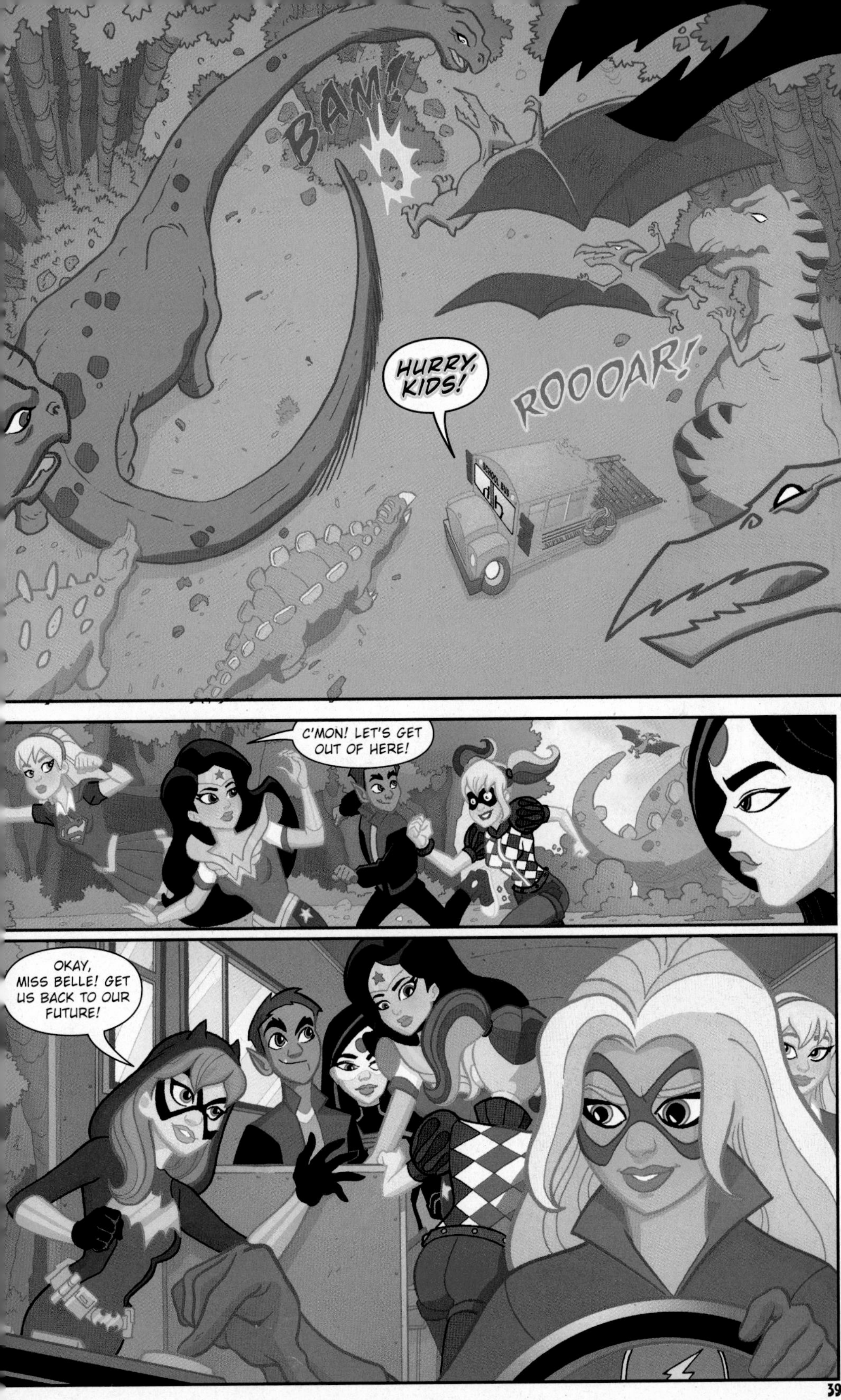
BAM!
HURRY, KIDS!
ROOOAR!
C'MON! LET'S GET OUT OF HERE!
OKAY, MISS BELLE! GET US BACK TO OUR FUTURE!

PL... unk!

OH SWEET LUCKY LINDBERGH! SUPER HERO HIGH IS STILL HERE!

I THOUGHT YOU KNEW WE WERE GOING TO BE "DUCKY."

I BETTER GET TO IT. A MESS LIKE THAT MEANS I'LL HAVE TO FILL OUT AN INCIDENT REPORT FOR PRINCIPAL WALLER.

TIME TRAVELING'S TRICKY BUSINESS. BEST NOT TO PUT OUT NEGATIVE VIBES WHEN YOU'RE IN THE TIME VORTEX!

ALL'S WELL THAT ENDS WELL, RIGHT, BATS?

YEP.

I THOUGHT FOR SURE SOMETHING WE DID IN THE PAST WOULD MAKE MODERN HUMANS HAVE LIZARD TONGUES, OR A THIRD EYE--

WAIT, YOU GUYS DON'T ALREADY HAVE THOSE?

OR WEBBED TOES!

HA HA HA HA HA!

CHAPTER THREE

SAVAGE HIGH

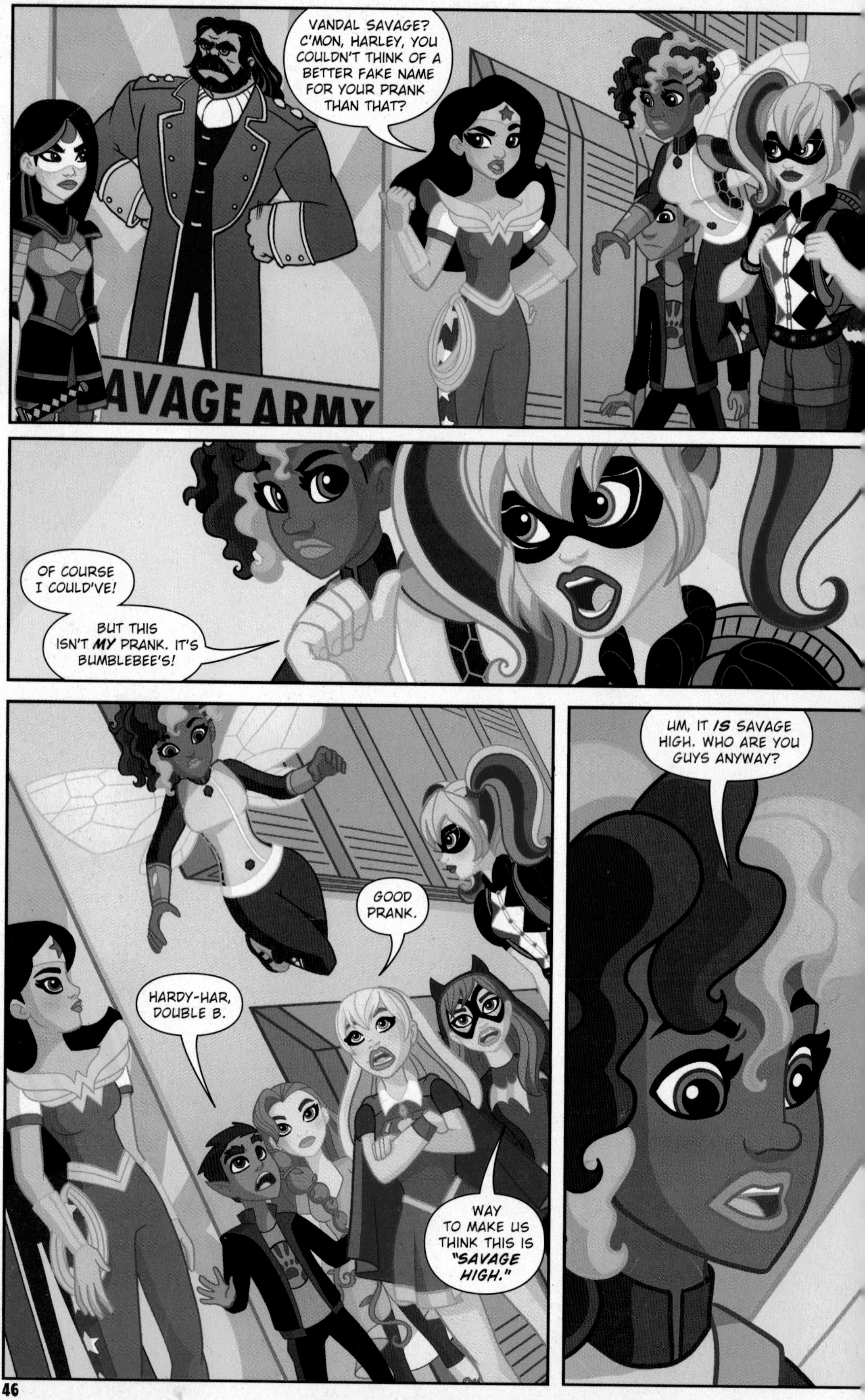
VANDAL SAVAGE? C'MON, HARLEY, YOU COULDN'T THINK OF A BETTER FAKE NAME FOR YOUR PRANK THAN THAT?
AVAGE ARMY
OF COURSE I COULD'VE!
BUT THIS ISN'T *MY* PRANK. IT'S BUMBLEBEE'S!
GOOD PRANK.
HARDY-HAR, DOUBLE B.
WAY TO MAKE US THINK THIS IS *"SAVAGE HIGH."*
UM, IT *IS* SAVAGE HIGH. WHO ARE YOU GUYS ANYWAY?

FOR THE LOVE OF ARMPIT FARTS! YA *REALLY* DON'T KNOW *ANY* OF US?

SHE KIND OF LOOKS LIKE A GIRL NAMED POWER GIRL, WHO GOES TO SCHOOL HERE.

THE GREEN TEAM SEEMS MORE LIKE THE GOTHAM CITY PREP TYPE.

WAIT. AREN'T YOU THE GIRL WHO GOT EXPELLED LAST SEMESTER FOR PUTTING KABOOM CANDY IN PRINCIPAL SAVAGE'S COFFEE?

HA! NOT ME, BUT SOUNDS LIKE A GIRLIE AFTER MY OWN *HEART!*

47

I'VE *DEFINITELY* NEVER SEEN YOU BEFORE. WOULD'VE REMEMBERED THE TIARA.

BUMBLEBEE, IT'S *ME,* WONDER WOMAN. WE'RE BEST FRIENDS.

BEST FRIENDS?

BUT I DON'T HAVE *ANY* FRIENDS HERE.

THAT *SETTLES* IT! WE *HAVE* TO FIND MISS BELLE AND *FIX* THIS FUTURE!

HUH?

WOOP!

WOOP!

YEESH! THE CLASS BELL HERE SURE IS ANNOYIN'!

ANTI-SAVAGE INSURGENT IDENTIFIED ON SCHOOL GROUNDS. STUDENTS TO BATTLE STATIONS!

YOU GUYS *HAVE* TO GET OUT OF HERE!

ANTI-SAVAGE INSURGENT? THAT MUST BE MISS BELLE!

I'LL GET YOU TO SAFETY.

BUT WE *CAN'T* LEAVE MISS BELLE BEHIND!

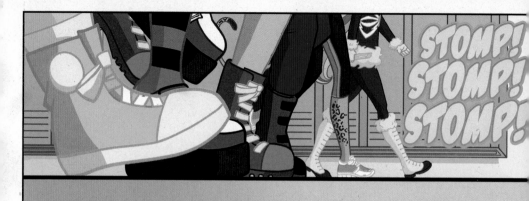

STOMP!
STOMP!
STOMP!

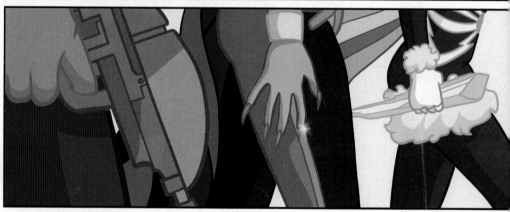

BUMBLEBEE! WHY AREN'T YOU GOING TO YOUR BATTLE STATION?

ON MY WAY, STAR SAPPHIRE!

BUT PRINCIPAL SAVAGE INSTRUCTED ME TO HANG HIS LATEST PROPAGANDA, I MEAN, *POSTER* FIRST.

PRINCIPAL SAVAGE INSTRUCTED? ALL RIGHT. AS YOU WERE.

HEY NOW, DOLLS! WHAT'S THE BIG IDEA?

THE BIG IDEA IS THAT YOU ORCHESTRATED A COUP AGAINST PRINCIPAL SAVAGE TWO MONTHS AGO!

YEAH, AND YOU JUST WALTZ IN HERE LIKE NOTHING HAPPENED.

GUESS THAT WAS REAL SILLY OF ME.

PRINCIPAL SAVAGE WILL BE WAITING FOR YOU IN INSURGENT DETENTION.

NO.

I HAVE TO HELP--

GO AFTER HER NOW, AND WE'LL ALL END UP IN DETENTION.

IF YOU WANT TO GET BACK TO YOUR RIGHT TIME-- WHICH SOUNDS LIKE A GOOD TIME TO ME--WE HAVE TO STRATEGIZE.

YOU'RE RIGHT, BUMBLEBEE. AS USUAL.

I'VE NEVER BEEN IN HERE BEFORE.

IN OUR TIME, WE USE IT FOR DETECTIVE CLUB MEETINGS.

HOW TO FIX TIME

DETECTIVE CLUB? SOUNDS AWESOME! PRINCIPAL SAVAGE STRONGLY DISCOURAGES ANY INVESTIGATIVE WORK.

HOW TO FIX TIME BRAINSTORM

ALL RIGHT, WHO HAS AN IDEA?

ME ME ME!

BEAST BOY?

FIRST, WE NEED SIX DOZEN EXTRA CHEESY PIZZAS.

OH! IF WE'RE ORDERING PIZZA, CAN I GET GARLIC KNOTS?

NO PIZZA!

JUST THE GARLIC KNOTS THEN?

TO FIX TIME, WE NEED LIBERTY BELLE AND THE TIME MACHINE. HERE'S THE PLAN--

FIX TIME BRAINSTORM

"--HARLEY AND I WILL RECOVER THE TIME MACHINE."

"BUMBLEBEE, YOU LEAD WONDER WOMAN, SUPERGIRL, BEAST BOY, KATANA, AND IVY TO INSURGENT DETENTION AND RELEASE MISS BELLE."

STUDENT I.D. RECOGNIZED.

CLEARANCE AUTHORIZED.

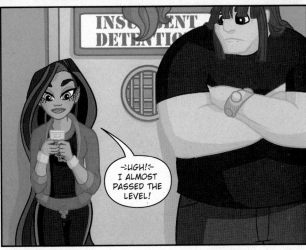

~UGH!~ I ALMOST PASSED THE LEVEL!

CHEETAH, WE'RE NOT SUPPOSED TO BE PLAYING GAMES WHILE ON DUTY.

SHUT IT, MAMMOTH!

HUH?

SHNK!

TRESPASSERS!

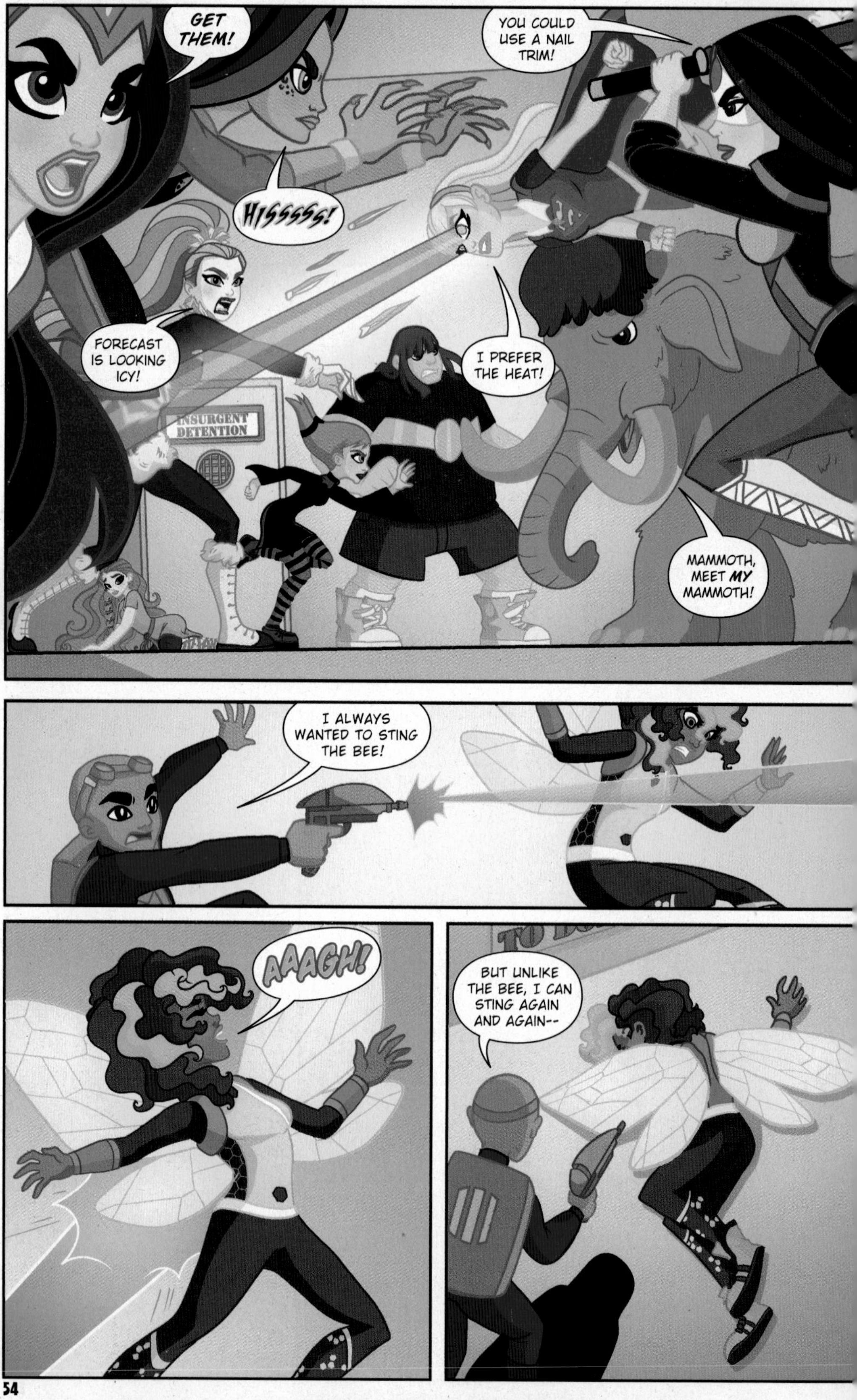
GET THEM!
YOU COULD USE A NAIL TRIM!
HISSSSS!
FORECAST IS LOOKING ICY!
I PREFER THE HEAT!
INSURGENT DETENTION
MAMMOTH, MEET *MY* MAMMOTH!
I ALWAYS WANTED TO STING THE BEE!
AAAGH!
BUT UNLIKE THE BEE, I CAN STING AGAIN AND AGAIN--

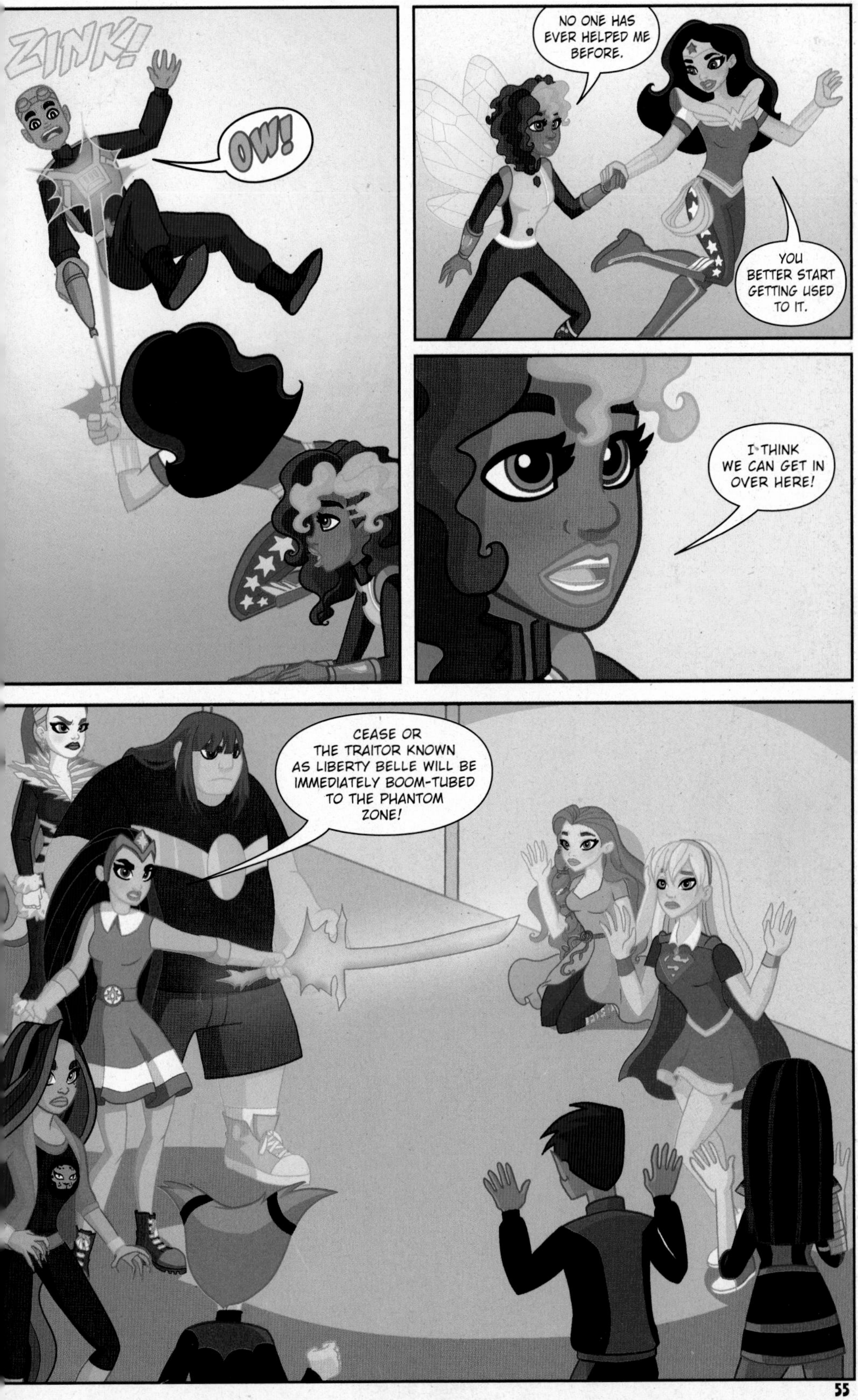
ZINK!
OW!
NO ONE HAS EVER HELPED ME BEFORE.
YOU BETTER START GETTING USED TO IT.
I THINK WE CAN GET IN OVER HERE!
CEASE OR THE TRAITOR KNOWN AS LIBERTY BELLE WILL BE IMMEDIATELY BOOM-TUBED TO THE PHANTOM ZONE!

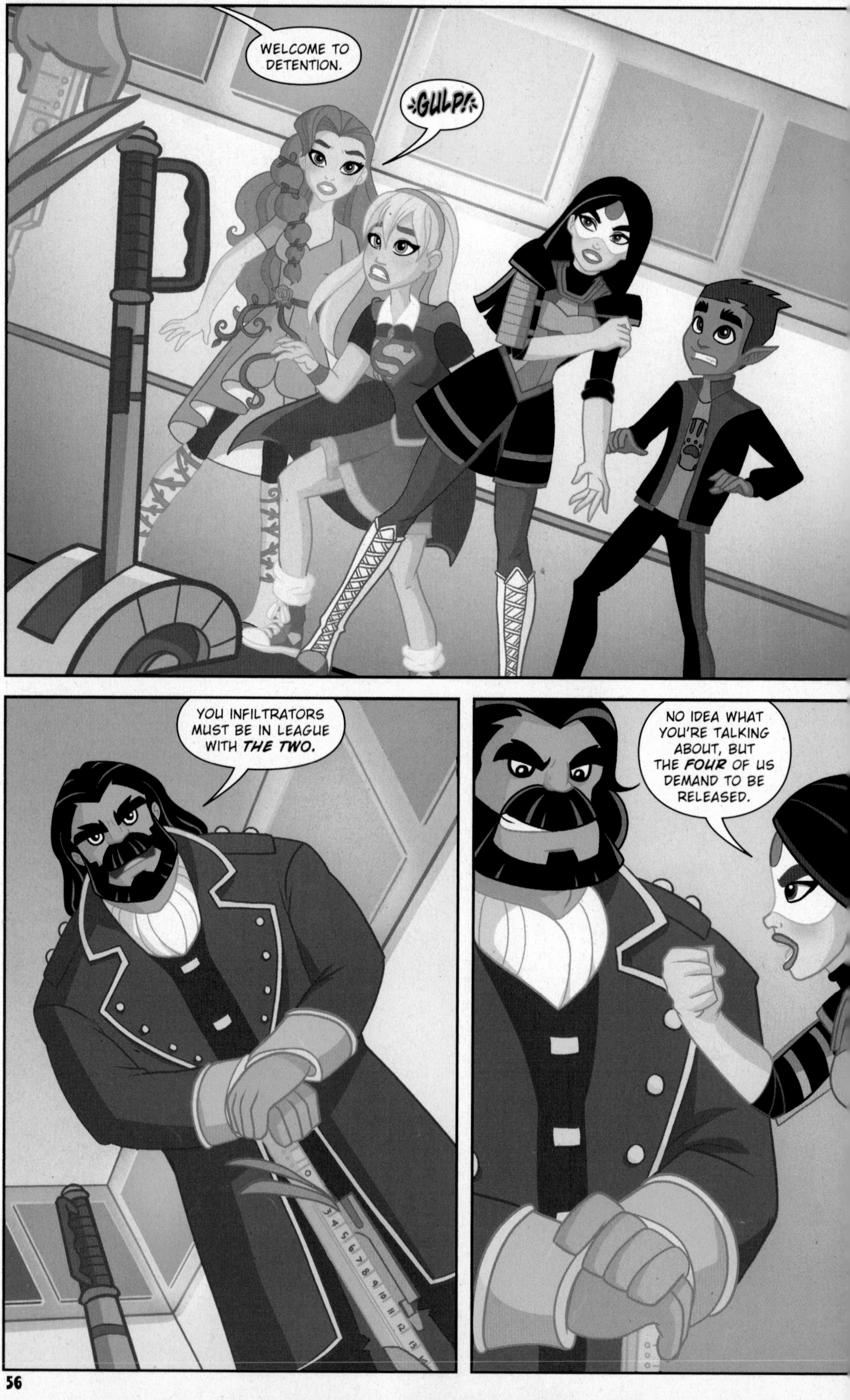
WELCOME TO DETENTION.
GULP!
YOU INFILTRATORS MUST BE IN LEAGUE WITH ***THE TWO.***
NO IDEA WHAT YOU'RE TALKING ABOUT, BUT THE ***FOUR*** OF US DEMAND TO BE RELEASED.

ZAAAP!

UNH!

SCARY DUDE'S RIGHT. I CAN'T EVEN GO CHIMP!

ALL YOUR STRENGTH AND POWERS ARE USELESS IN THIS ROOM.

WHERE ARE THE TWO?!

WE DON'T KNOW WHAT YOU'RE TALKING ABOUT.

IF YOU WON'T TALK TO ME ABOUT *THE TWO*, YOU WILL TALK TO MY FINEST INTERROGATOR. THE *DEMON* ETRIGAN.

CRICK CRACK!

PROFESSOR ETRIGAN?

BUT YOU DON'T DO THAT DEMON STUFF ANYMORE. YOU'RE A GOOD GUY!

HOW CAN YOUR WILD TALE OF REFORMATION BE TRUE, WHEN FOR CENTURIES IT'S BEEN VANDAL'S BIDDING I DO?

DID HE SAY *"CENTURIES"*?

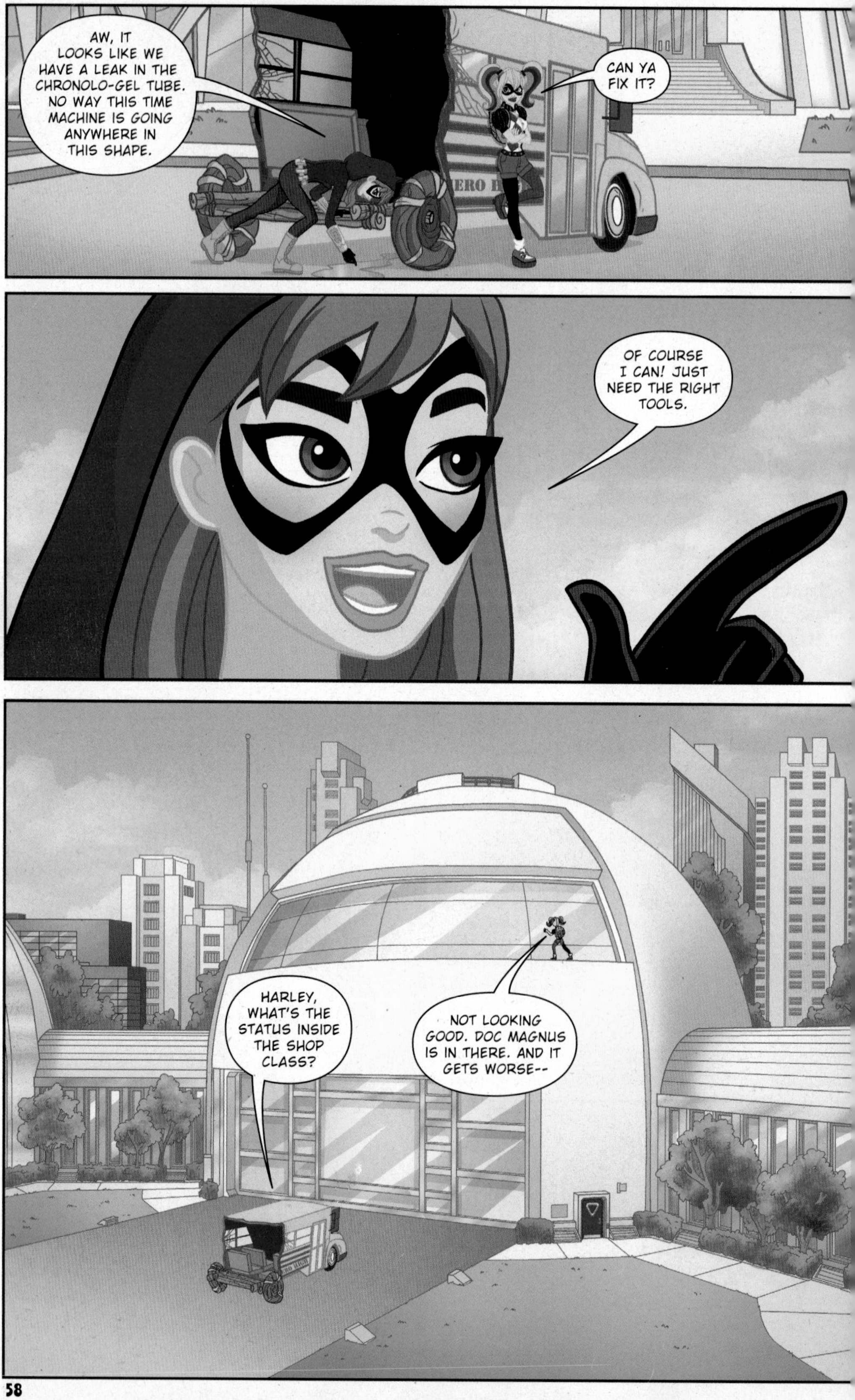
AW, IT LOOKS LIKE WE HAVE A LEAK IN THE CHRONOLO-GEL TUBE. NO WAY THIS TIME MACHINE IS GOING ANYWHERE IN THIS SHAPE.
CAN YA FIX IT?
OF COURSE I CAN! JUST NEED THE RIGHT TOOLS.
HARLEY, WHAT'S THE STATUS INSIDE THE SHOP CLASS?
NOT LOOKING GOOD. DOC MAGNUS IS IN THERE. AND IT GETS WORSE--

HE'S MADE SOME UNFORTUNATE FACIAL HAIR DECISIONS.

WE'LL NEED TO CREATE A DISTRACTION TO GET HIM OUTTA THERE.

THIS TIMELINE'S HARLEY GAVE ME A REAL POPPIN' IDEA!

MECHANICS, ROBOTICS, AND AUTOMOTIVE WORKSHOP

KABOOM CANDY

SODER COLA

FIRE IN THE HOLE!

SODER COLA

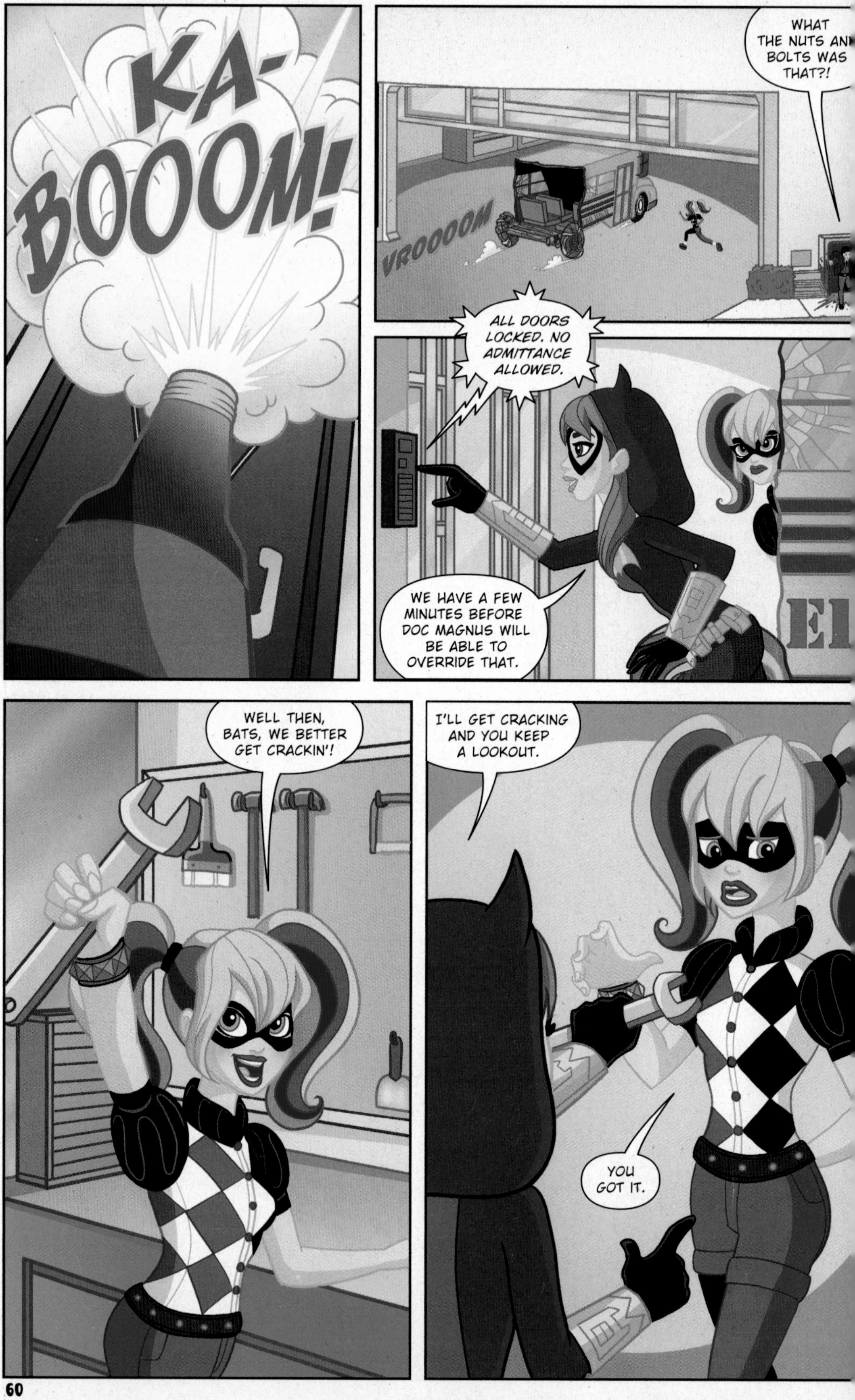
KA-BOOOM!
VROOOOM
WHAT THE NUTS AN BOLTS WAS THAT?!
ALL DOORS LOCKED. NO ADMITTANCE ALLOWED.
WE HAVE A FEW MINUTES BEFORE DOC MAGNUS WILL BE ABLE TO OVERRIDE THAT.
WELL THEN, BATS, WE BETTER GET CRACKIN'!
I'LL GET CRACKING AND YOU KEEP A LOOKOUT.
YOU GOT IT.

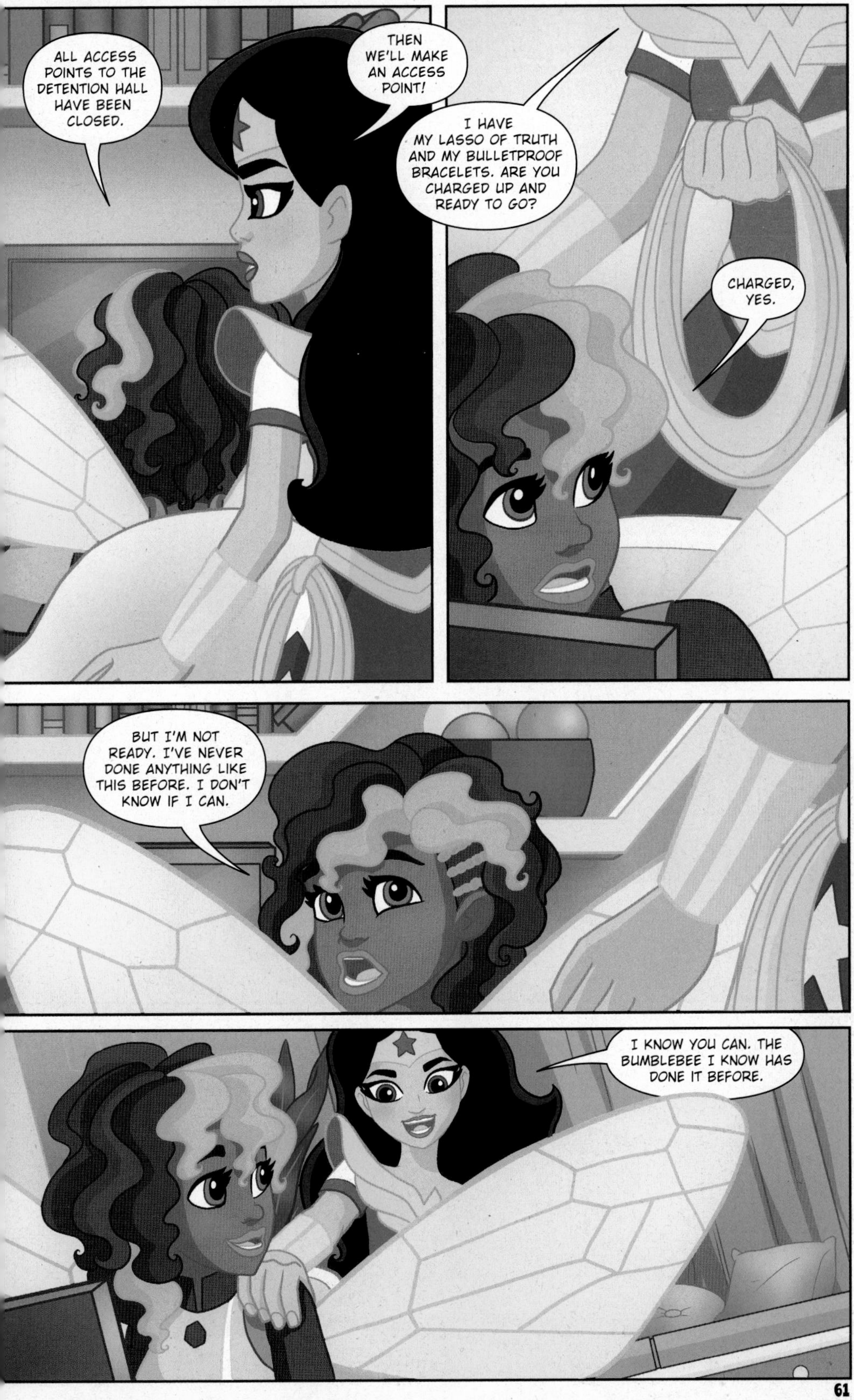
ALL ACCESS POINTS TO THE DETENTION HALL HAVE BEEN CLOSED.
THEN WE'LL MAKE AN ACCESS POINT!
I HAVE MY LASSO OF TRUTH AND MY BULLETPROOF BRACELETS. ARE YOU CHARGED UP AND READY TO GO?
CHARGED, YES.
BUT I'M NOT READY. I'VE NEVER DONE ANYTHING LIKE THIS BEFORE. I DON'T KNOW IF I CAN.
I KNOW YOU CAN. THE BUMBLEBEE I KNOW HAS DONE IT BEFORE.

YOU'RE CAPABLE OF AMAZING THINGS. I'VE SEEN YOU STAND UP AGAINST GIGANTA, SOLOMON GRUNDY AND CROC!

NO WAY! I TOOK DOWN CROC?

HE WAS TRYING TO STEAL A TUNA SANDWICH FROM THE CAPES & COWLS CAFÉ AND YOU STOPPED HIM BEFORE HE EVEN KNEW WHAT HIT HIM!

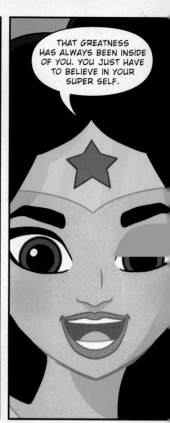

THAT GREATNESS HAS ALWAYS BEEN INSIDE OF YOU. YOU JUST HAVE TO BELIEVE IN YOUR SUPER SELF.

BELIEVE IN MY SUPER SELF.

THEY CUT OFF ALL REGULAR ACCESS, BUT THEY DIDN'T COUNT ON A BEE-SIZED HERO.

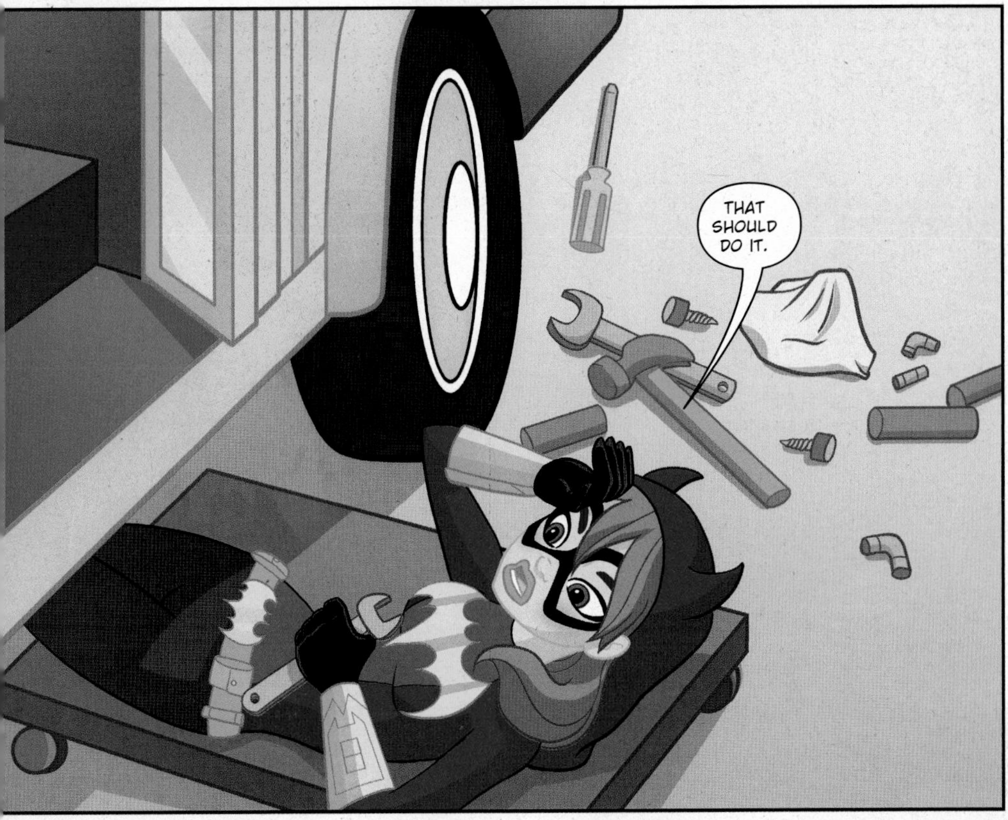
THAT SHOULD DO IT.

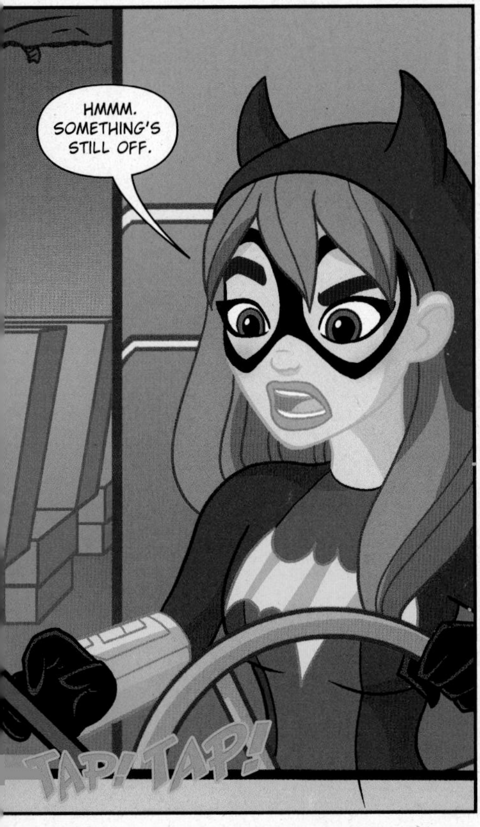
HMMM. SOMETHING'S STILL OFF.
TAP! TAP!

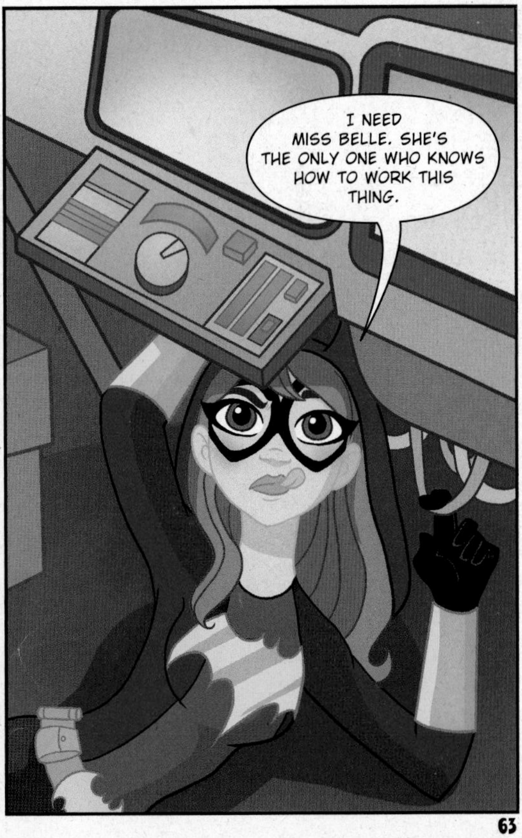
I NEED MISS BELLE. SHE'S THE ONLY ONE WHO KNOWS HOW TO WORK THIS THING.

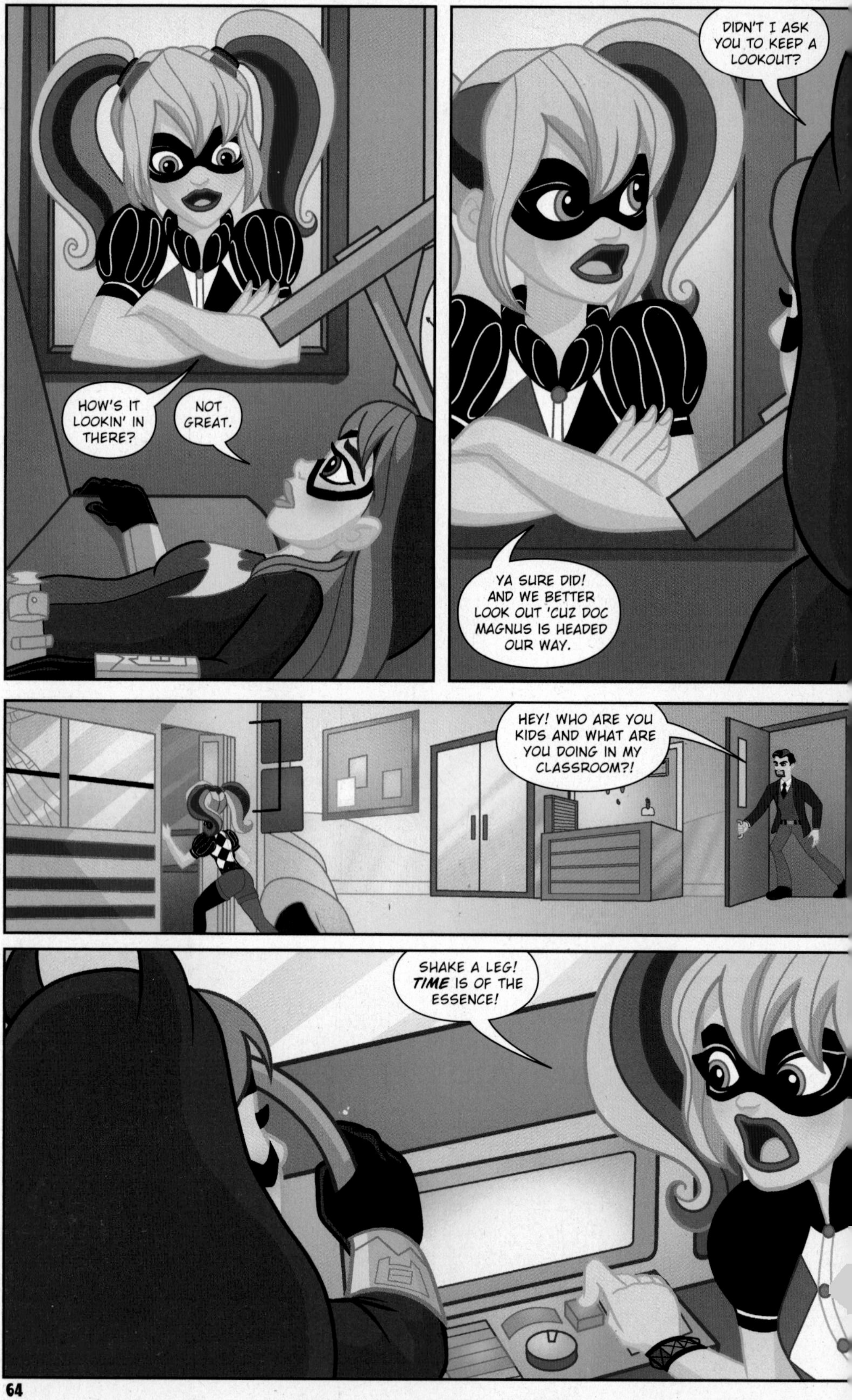
HOW'S IT LOOKIN' IN THERE?
NOT GREAT.
DIDN'T I ASK YOU TO KEEP A LOOKOUT?
YA SURE DID! AND WE BETTER LOOK OUT 'CUZ DOC MAGNUS IS HEADED OUR WAY.
HEY! WHO ARE YOU KIDS AND WHAT ARE YOU DOING IN MY CLASSROOM?!
SHAKE A LEG! **TIME** IS OF THE ESSENCE!

CHAPTER FOUR

HARLEY & BATGIRL'S EXCELLENT ADVENTURE

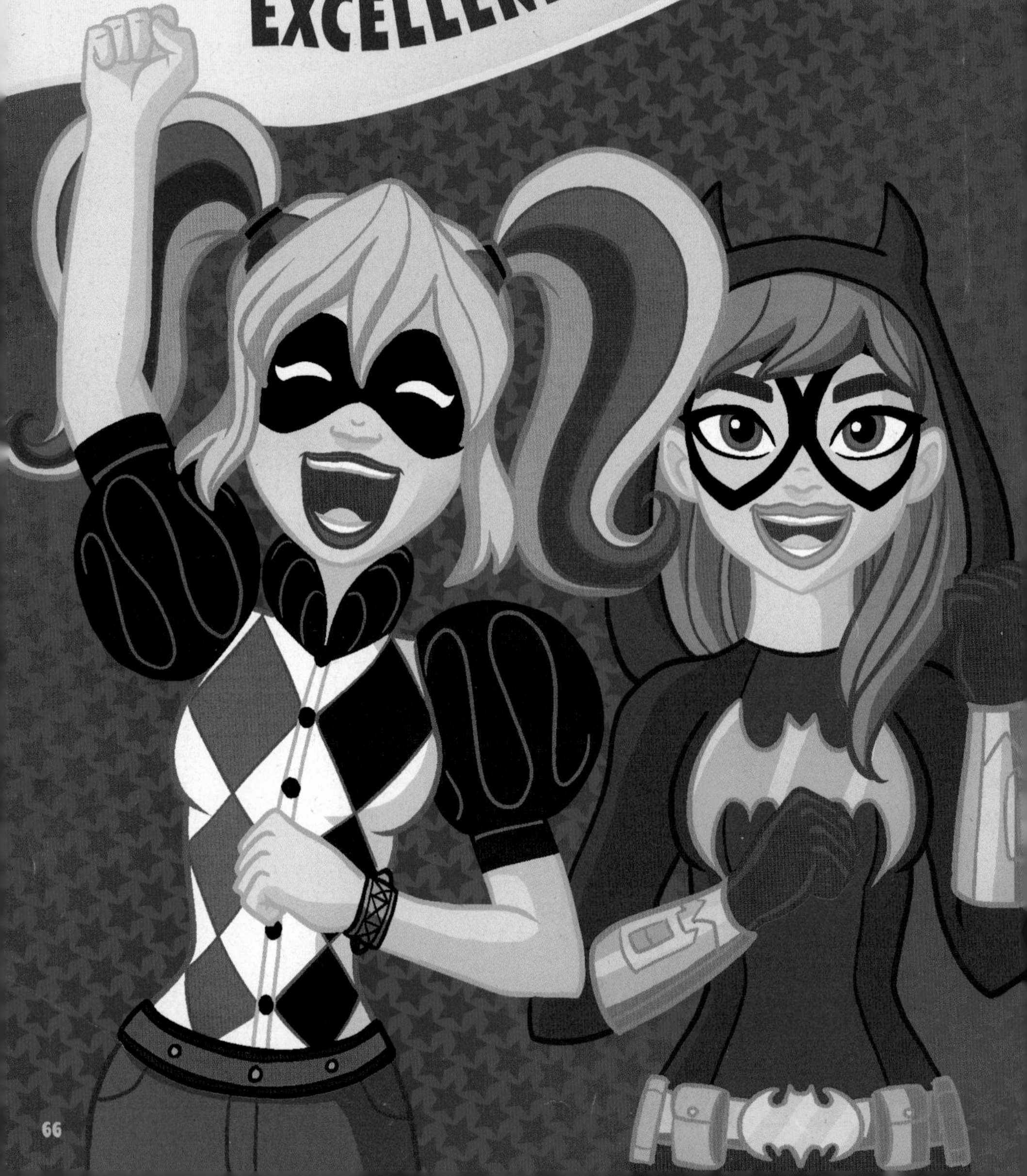

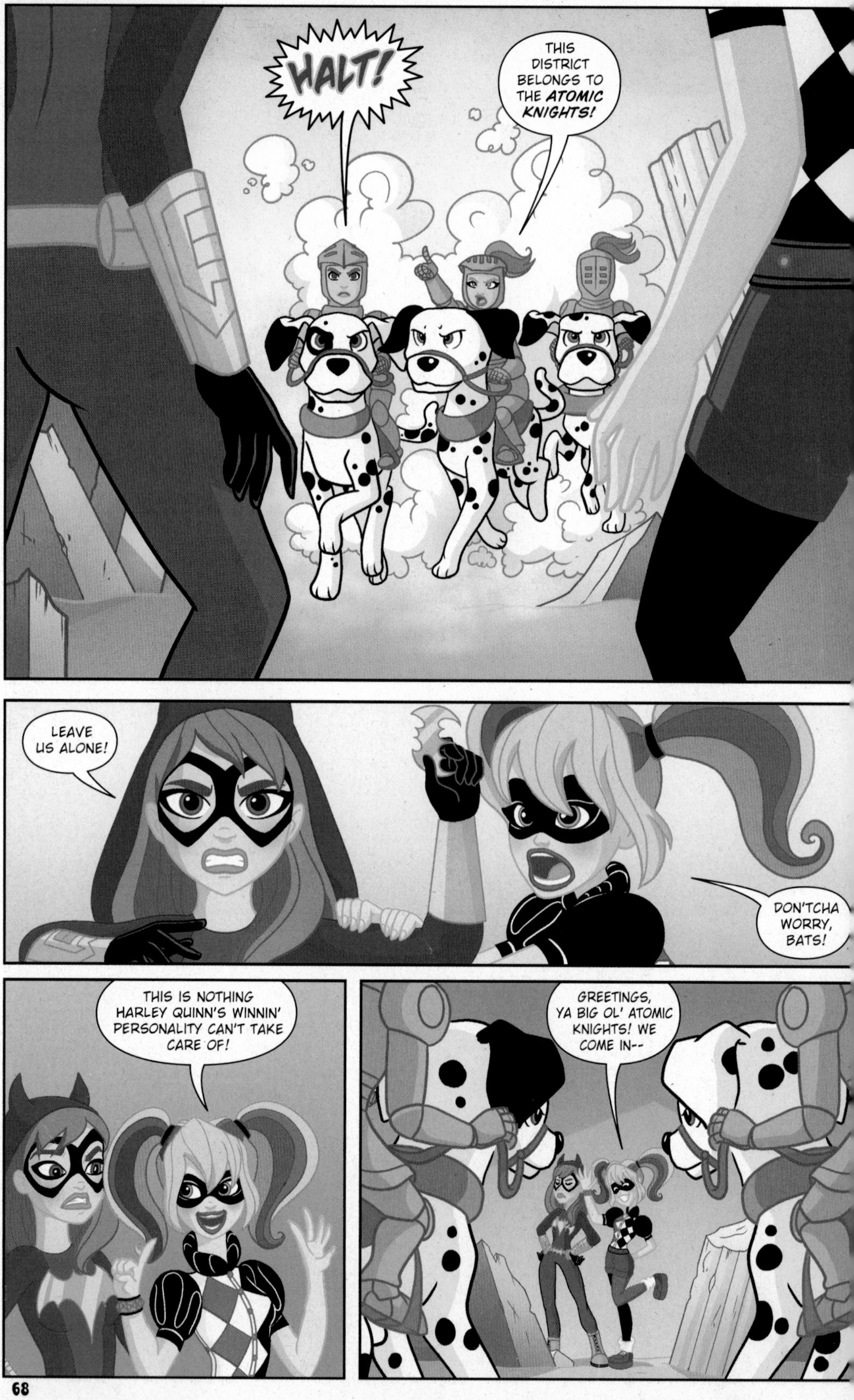
HALT!
THIS DISTRICT BELONGS TO THE ATOMIC KNIGHTS!
LEAVE US ALONE!
DON'TCHA WORRY, BATS!
THIS IS NOTHING HARLEY QUINN'S WINNIN' PERSONALITY CAN'T TAKE CARE OF!
GREETINGS, YA BIG OL' ATOMIC KNIGHTS! WE COME IN--

I HAVE A HANDCUFF-LOCK PICKER IN MY UTILITY BELT.

WE FOUND THESE GIRLS IN THE UNAUTHORIZED ZONE.

JUST DON'T TIP THEM OFF UNTIL WE'RE READY TO FIGHT OUR WAY OUT.

THEY DON'T HAVE HOLO-PERMITS OR I.D. CHIPS.

CLICK!

WE MUST ASSUME THE TRESPASSERS ARE SPIES FOR VANDAL SAVAGE!

WE'RE NOT O STINKIN' SPIES! ANDAL SAVAGE IS THE FELLA WE'RE TRYING TO STOP!

SHE ESCAPED THE HANDCUFFS?!

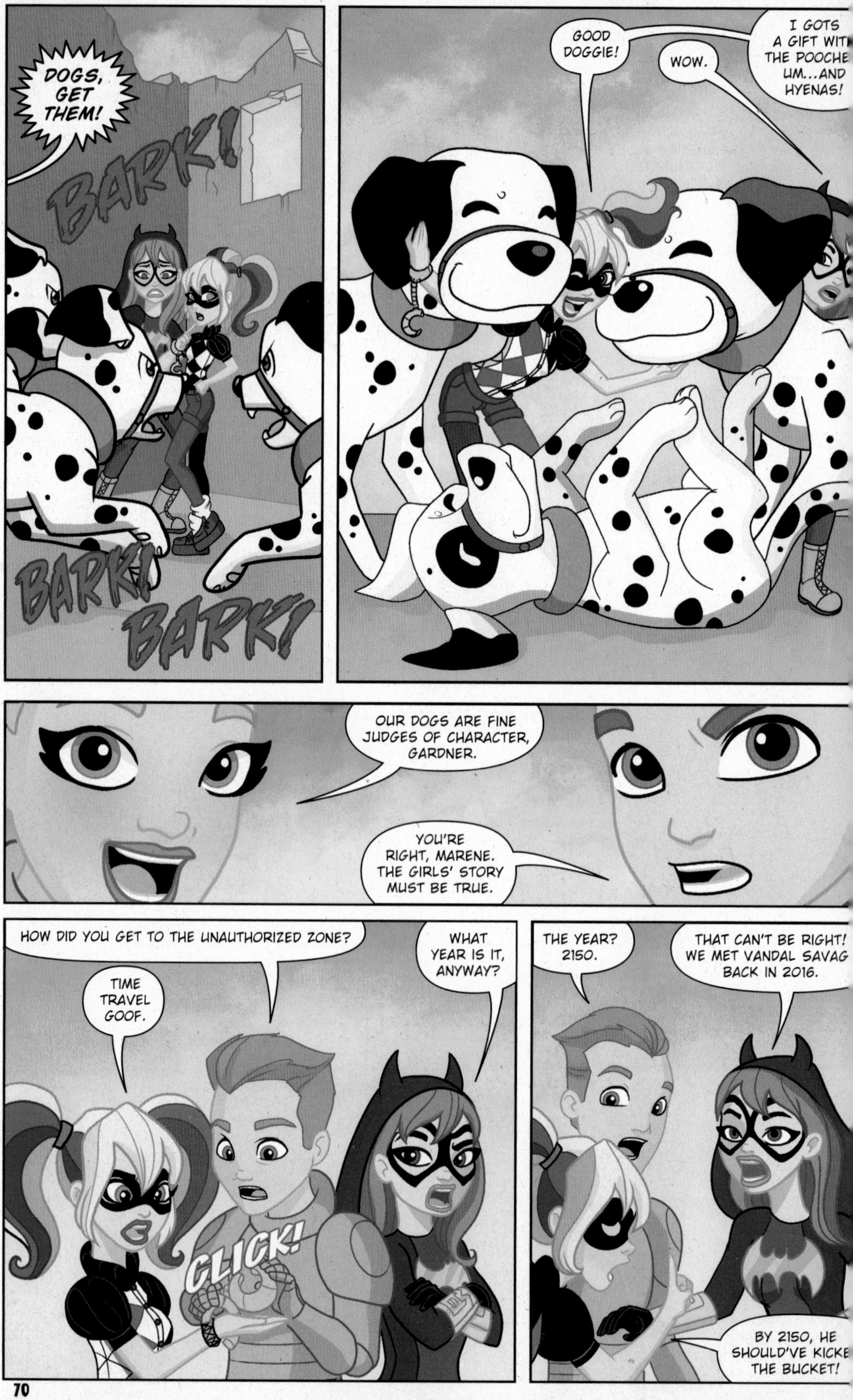
DOGS, GET THEM!
BARK!
BARK!
BARK!
GOOD DOGGIE!
WOW.
I GOTS A GIFT WIT THE POOCHE UM...AND HYENAS!
OUR DOGS ARE FINE JUDGES OF CHARACTER, GARDNER.
YOU'RE RIGHT, MARENE. THE GIRLS' STORY MUST BE TRUE.
HOW DID YOU GET TO THE UNAUTHORIZED ZONE?
TIME TRAVEL GOOF.
WHAT YEAR IS IT, ANYWAY?
CLICK!
THE YEAR? 2150.
THAT CAN'T BE RIGHT! WE MET VANDAL SAVAG BACK IN 2016.
BY 2150, HE SHOULD'VE KICKE THE BUCKET!

YOU REALLY DON'T KNOW? YOU'VE NEVER SEEN THE HOLO-STORY?

SEEN IT? I DON'T EVEN KNOW WHAT IT IS!

FOR YEARS, THIS STORY PLAYED ON EVERY HOLO-VISION THROUGHOUT THE GALAXY.

THE GRAND STORY OF VANDAL SAVAGE

VANDAL SAVAGE WAS THE GREATEST CAVEMAN WHO EVER LIVED!

OVER FIFTY THOUSAND YEARS AGO, THE BRIGHT AND CUNNING VANDAL SAVAGE SAW A METEORITE FALL FROM THE SKY.

ATTACK! USE ALL YOUR SUPER-POWERS!

THE WEAK INSURGENTS FOOLISHLY FOUGHT, BUT THEY WERE CRUSHED BY THE STRENGTH AND POWER OF THE SAVAGE ARMY.

VANDAL SAVAGE, THE GALAXY'S GREATEST EMPEROR!

ALL HAIL EMPEROR VANDAL SAVAGE!

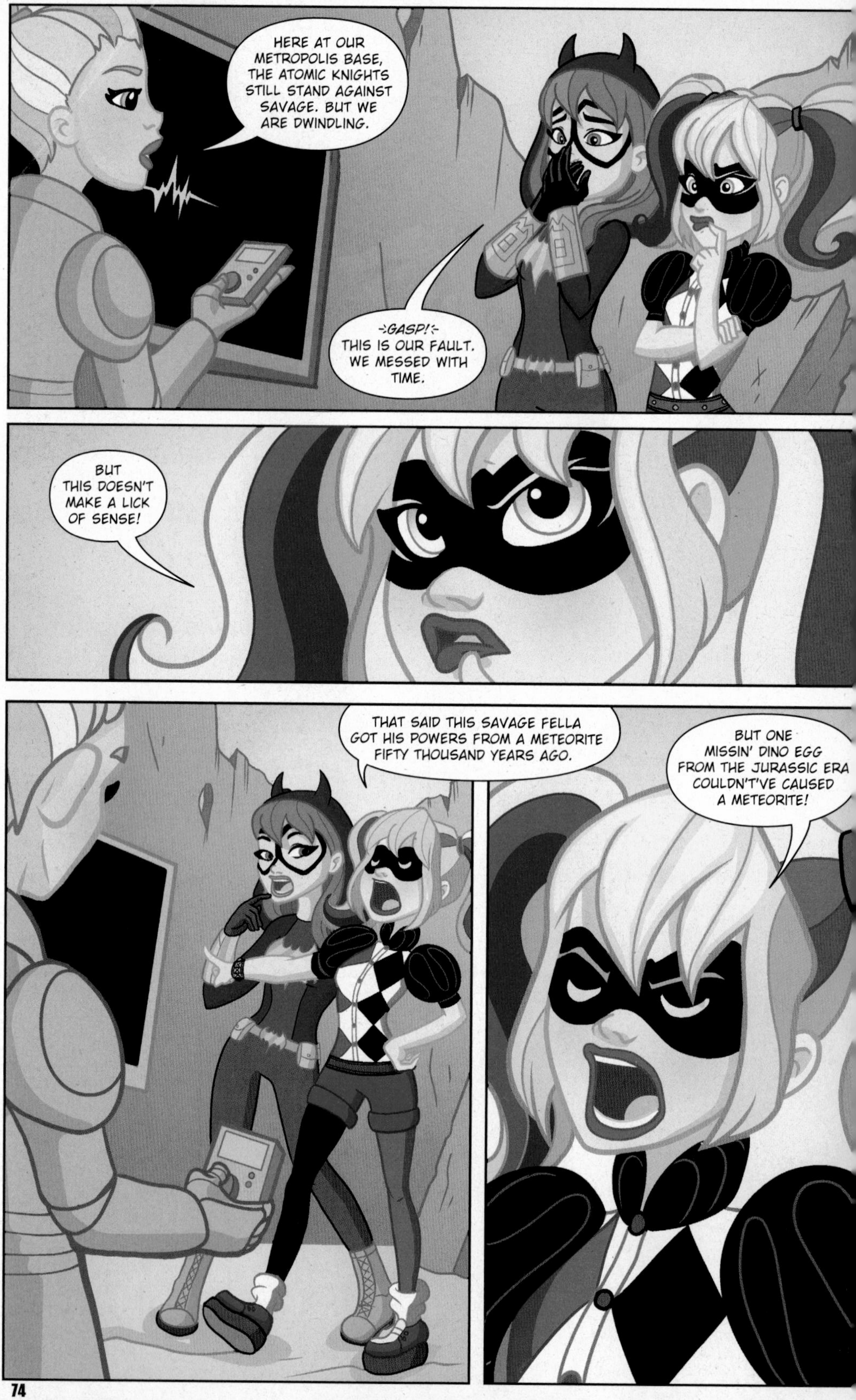
HERE AT OUR METROPOLIS BASE, THE ATOMIC KNIGHTS STILL STAND AGAINST SAVAGE. BUT WE ARE DWINDLING.
-GASP!- THIS IS OUR FAULT. WE MESSED WITH TIME.
BUT THIS DOESN'T MAKE A LICK OF SENSE!
THAT SAID THIS SAVAGE FELLA GOT HIS POWERS FROM A METEORITE FIFTY THOUSAND YEARS AGO.
BUT ONE MISSIN' DINO EGG FROM THE JURASSIC ERA COULDN'T'VE CAUSED A METEORITE!

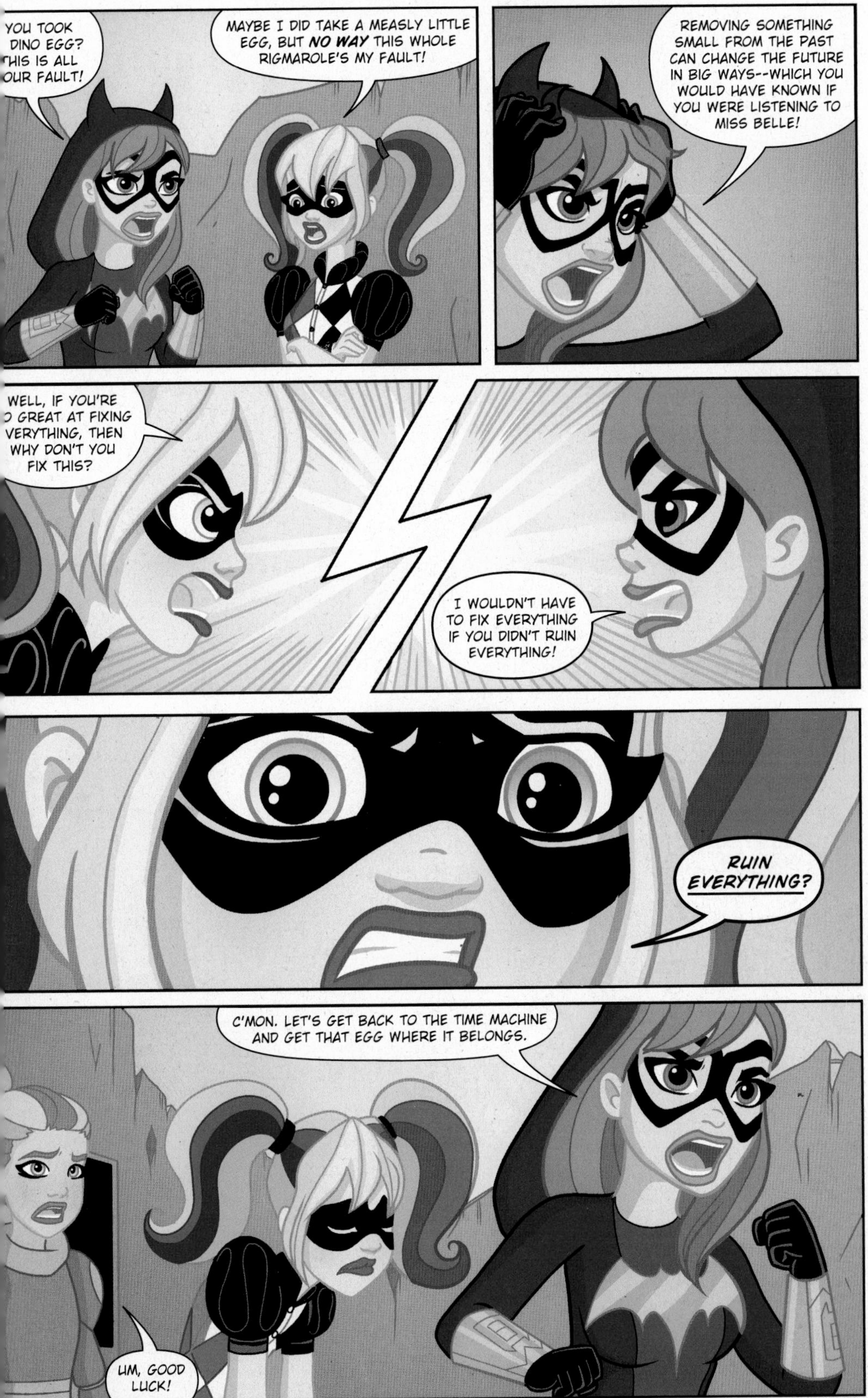

YOU TOOK DINO EGG? THIS IS ALL OUR FAULT!
MAYBE I DID TAKE A MEASLY LITTLE EGG, BUT NO WAY THIS WHOLE RIGMAROLE'S MY FAULT!
REMOVING SOMETHING SMALL FROM THE PAST CAN CHANGE THE FUTURE IN BIG WAYS--WHICH YOU WOULD HAVE KNOWN IF YOU WERE LISTENING TO MISS BELLE!
WELL, IF YOU'RE GREAT AT FIXING VERYTHING, THEN WHY DON'T YOU FIX THIS?
I WOULDN'T HAVE TO FIX EVERYTHING IF YOU DIDN'T RUIN EVERYTHING!
RUIN EVERYTHING?
C'MON. LET'S GET BACK TO THE TIME MACHINE AND GET THAT EGG WHERE IT BELONGS.
UM, GOOD LUCK!

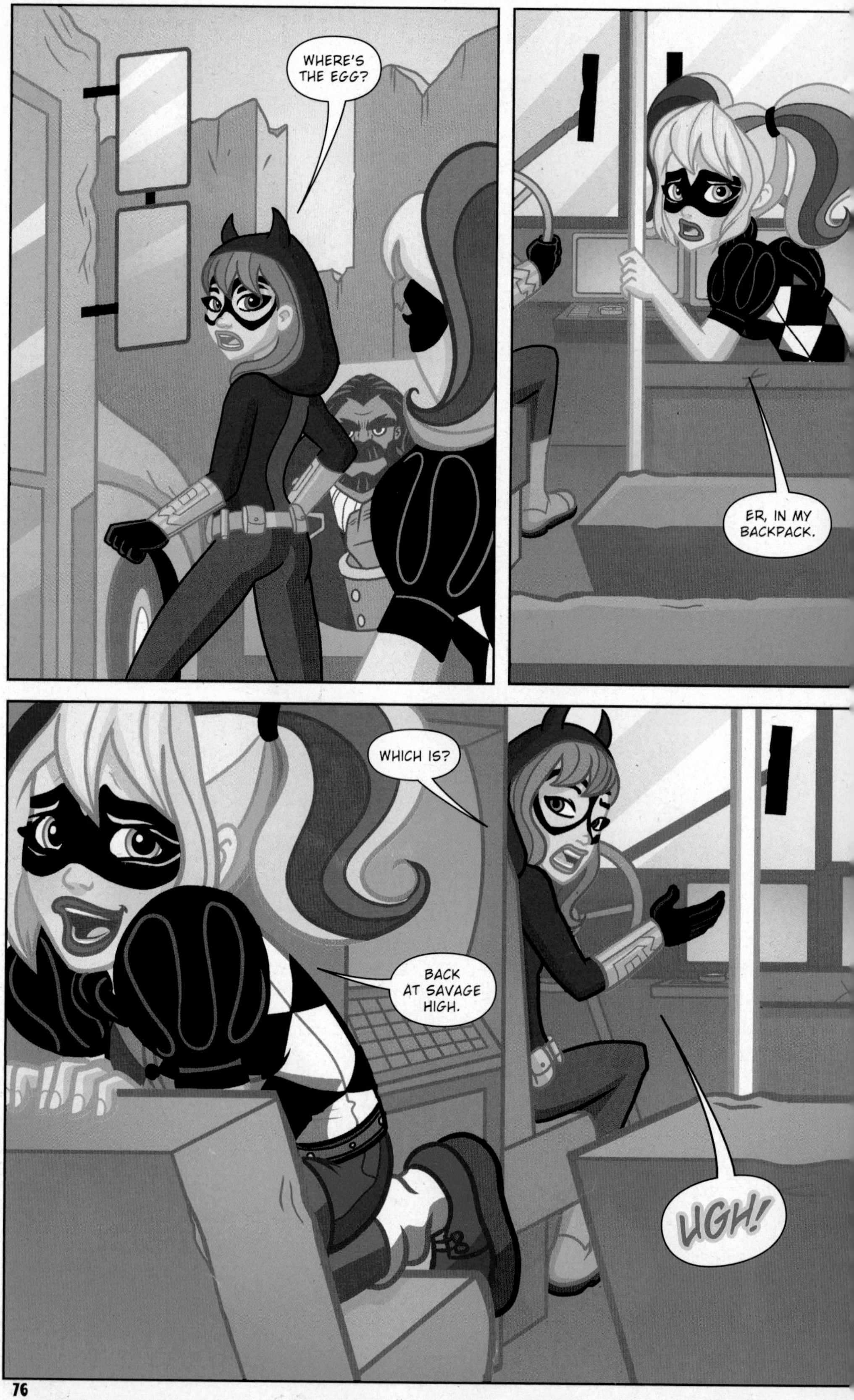
WHERE'S THE EGG?
ER, IN MY BACKPACK.
WHICH IS?
BACK AT SAVAGE HIGH.
UGH!

WE'LL GO BACK TO SAVAGE HIGH, GET THAT EGG, AND FIX THE PAST, ONCE AND FOR ALL.

SCHOOL BUS

1950 A.D.

1940 A.D.

1914.

HERO HIGH

THIS DOESN'T LOOK RIGHT.

NO SAVAGE HIGH HERE.

HEY! YOUR JALOPY CUT DOWN MY KITE!

WAIT A TICK--AREN'T YOU AMELIA EARHART?

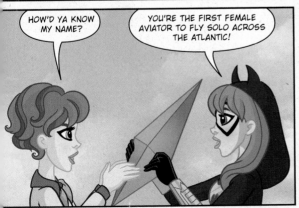

HOW'D YA KNOW MY NAME?

YOU'RE THE FIRST FEMALE AVIATOR TO FLY SOLO ACROSS THE ATLANTIC!

FLYIN' PLANES? HA! EVERYBODY KNOWS THAT GIRLS CAN'T FLY PLANES.

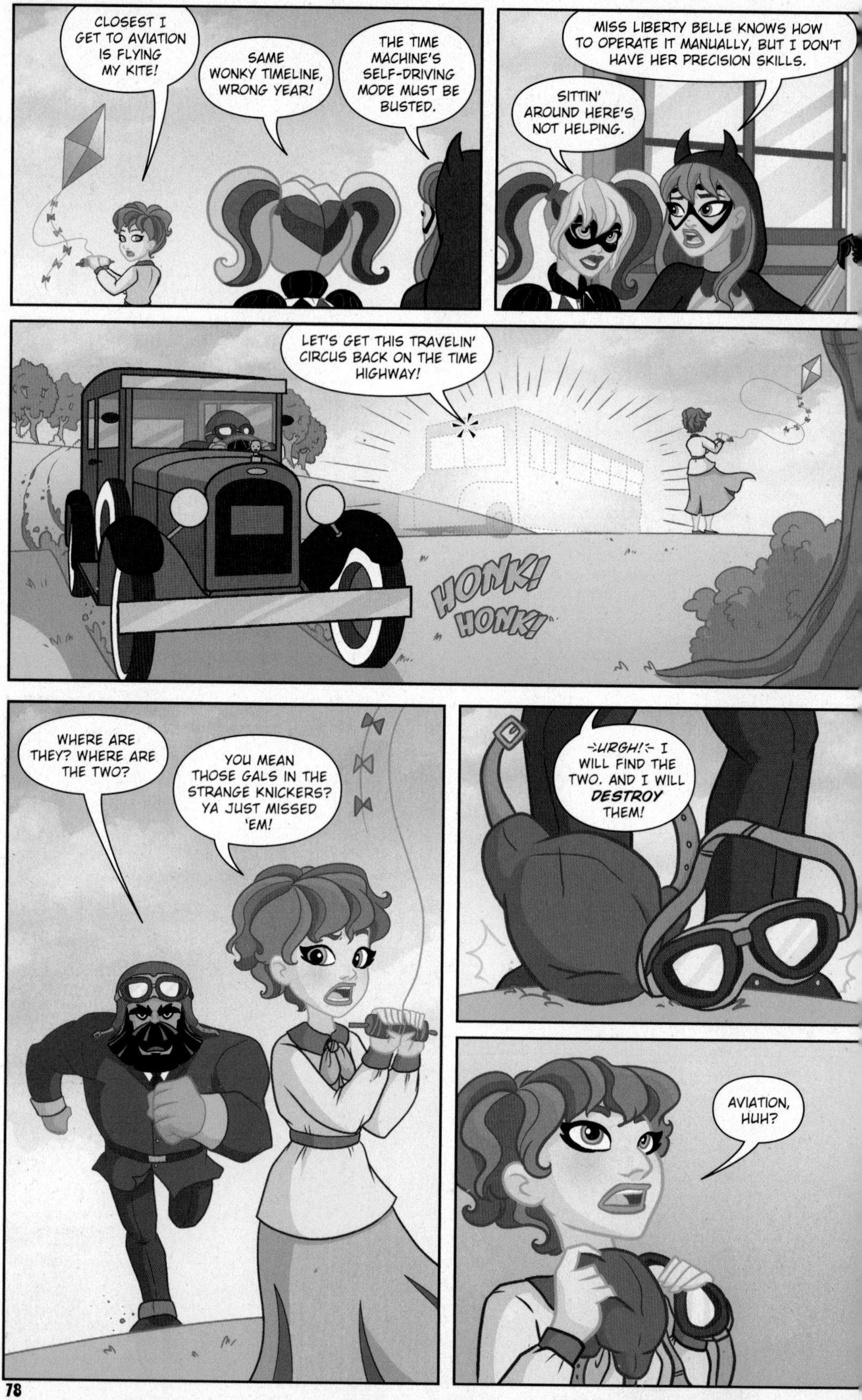
CLOSEST I GET TO AVIATION IS FLYING MY KITE!
SAME WONKY TIMELINE, WRONG YEAR!
THE TIME MACHINE'S SELF-DRIVING MODE MUST BE BUSTED.
MISS LIBERTY BELLE KNOWS HOW TO OPERATE IT MANUALLY, BUT I DON'T HAVE HER PRECISION SKILLS.
SITTIN' AROUND HERE'S NOT HELPING.
LET'S GET THIS TRAVELIN' CIRCUS BACK ON THE TIME HIGHWAY!
HONK! HONK!
WHERE ARE THEY? WHERE ARE THE TWO?
YOU MEAN THOSE GALS IN THE STRANGE KNICKERS? YA JUST MISSED 'EM!
URGH! I WILL FIND THE TWO. AND I WILL DESTROY THEM!
AVIATION, HUH?

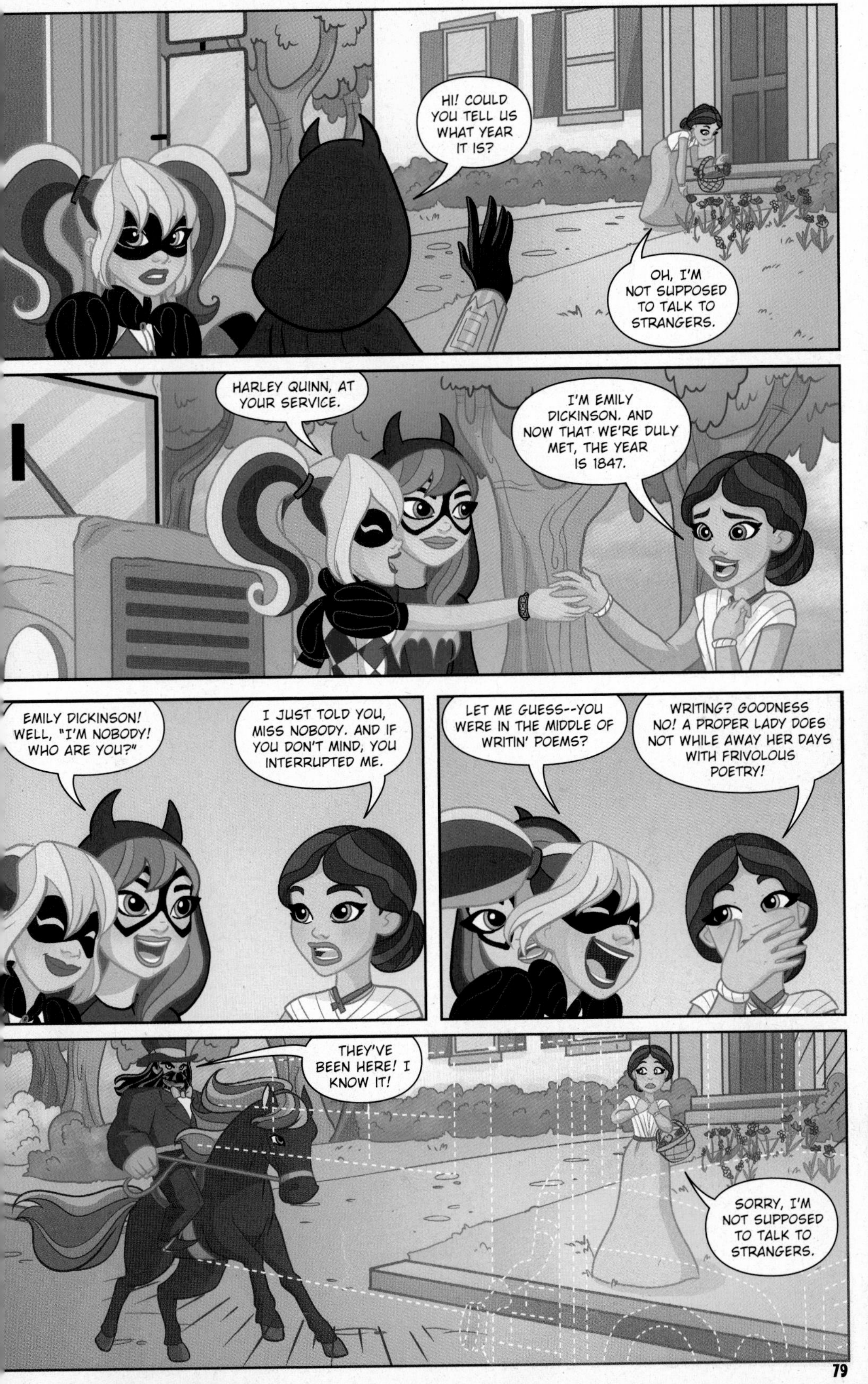
HI! COULD YOU TELL US WHAT YEAR IT IS?
OH, I'M NOT SUPPOSED TO TALK TO STRANGERS.
HARLEY QUINN, AT YOUR SERVICE.
I'M EMILY DICKINSON. AND NOW THAT WE'RE DULY MET, THE YEAR IS 1847.
EMILY DICKINSON! WELL, "I'M NOBODY! WHO ARE YOU?"
I JUST TOLD YOU, MISS NOBODY. AND IF YOU DON'T MIND, YOU INTERRUPTED ME.
LET ME GUESS--YOU WERE IN THE MIDDLE OF WRITIN' POEMS?
WRITING? GOODNESS NO! A PROPER LADY DOES NOT WHILE AWAY HER DAYS WITH FRIVOLOUS POETRY!
THEY'VE BEEN HERE! I KNOW IT!
SORRY, I'M NOT SUPPOSED TO TALK TO STRANGERS.

SORRY, WE'RE IN THE WRONG PLACE.

ACTUALLY, RIGHT PLACE, WRONG TIME.

YOU SHOULD PROBABLY FORGET THIS EVER HAPPENED!

THEY APPEARED OUT OF THIN AIR AND VANISHED THE SAME. WE CALL THEM "THE TWO."*

*TRANSLATED FROM WYANDOT.

HA! ANOTHER SILLY MYTH! NO GIRLS COULD HAVE POWERS THAT EXCEED MINE.

PLEASE DON'T TOUCH ANYTHING. I CAN'T RISK ANYTHING ELSE GOING WRONG.

SURE THING, BATS. I *KNOW* WE'LL GET TO THE RIGHT TIME...ONE OF THESE TIMES!

WHEN DO YOU THINK WE ARE?

WITCHES! **BURN** THEM!

WHENEVER IT IS, IT'S TIME TO GET OUT OF HERE!

THE TWO? THE OLD LEGEND IS TRUE!

GET THE WITCHES!

THEY DISAPPEARED!

ALL YE STAY BACK, LEST YE TOUCH THEIR WITCHY RESIDUE!

THE TWO MUST BE IMMORTAL LIKE ME. I WILL FIND THE SOURCE OF THEIR POWERS AND TAKE IT FOR MYSELF!

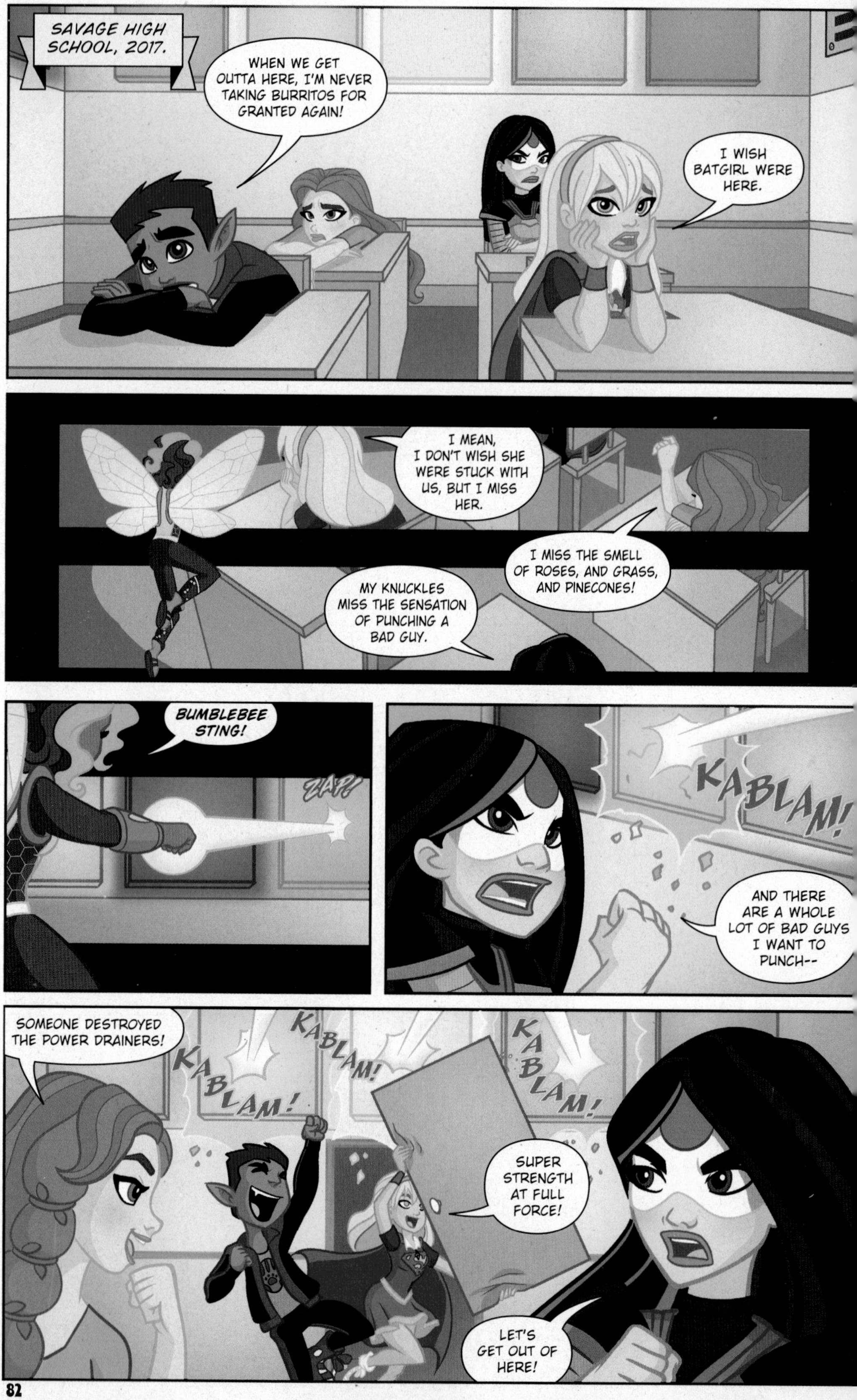
SAVAGE HIGH SCHOOL, 2017.
WHEN WE GET OUTTA HERE, I'M NEVER TAKING BURRITOS FOR GRANTED AGAIN!
I WISH BATGIRL WERE HERE.
I MEAN, I DON'T WISH SHE WERE STUCK WITH US, BUT I MISS HER.
I MISS THE SMELL OF ROSES, AND GRASS, AND PINECONES!
MY KNUCKLES MISS THE SENSATION OF PUNCHING A BAD GUY.
BUMBLEBEE STING!
ZAP!
KABLAM!
AND THERE ARE A WHOLE LOT OF BAD GUYS I WANT TO PUNCH--
SOMEONE DESTROYED THE POWER DRAINERS!
KABLAM!
KABLAM!
KABLAM!
SUPER STRENGTH AT FULL FORCE!
LET'S GET OUT OF HERE!

GROAN!

WONDER WOMAN, YOU SAVED US!

NOT ME-- IT WAS BUMBLEBEE WHO DID THE HARD PART.

HEY!

AW, IT WAS JUST A LITTLE -ETTING LITTLE AND A FEW ELECTRIC STINGS!

WAY TO GO, DOUBLE B!

YOU'RE BETTER THAN BEGONIAS!

ÜBERFLY MOVES, GIRL!

C'MON! YOUR TEACHER WILL BE THIS WAY.

WE'RE COMING, MISS BELLE!

"A FOUR-LETTER WORD FOR SANDWICH..."

HMMM... HERO!

PLUNK!

HEY! THIS IS METROPOLIS!

WE'RE GETTING CLOSE.

BUT JUDGING BY THE BEATS ON THE BOOM BOX, I'D SAY LATE 1980s.

ARE YA SEEIN' WHAT I'M SEEIN'? THAT'S WEE WALLABY!

PRINCIPAL WALLER?

SOLOMON GRUNDY, BORN ON A MONDAY--

--AAGH!-- MONSTER!

NO, HARLEY! WE CAN'T INTERFERE!

WE GOTTA HELP HER! THAT'S WHAT SHE TAUGHT US TO DO!

BUT SHE *HASN'T* TAUGHT US THAT IN THE 1980s.

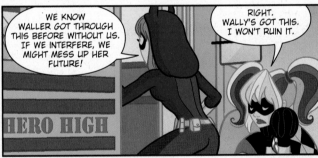

WE KNOW WALLER GOT THROUGH THIS BEFORE WITHOUT US. IF WE INTERFERE, WE MIGHT MESS UP HER FUTURE!

RIGHT. WALLY'S GOT THIS. I WON'T RUIN IT.

HERO HIGH

HELP! SOMEONE, HELP!

GRUNDY GET GIRL!

WE MADE IT TO SAVAGE HIGH!

HIGH

PLUNK!

WE'LL HAVE THIS TIME TROUBLE FIXED IN A FLASH!

THE TWO! I'VE BEEN TRACKING YOU FOR CENTURIES, BUT NOW YOUR TIME IS UP!

CHAPTER FIVE

EGGING ON

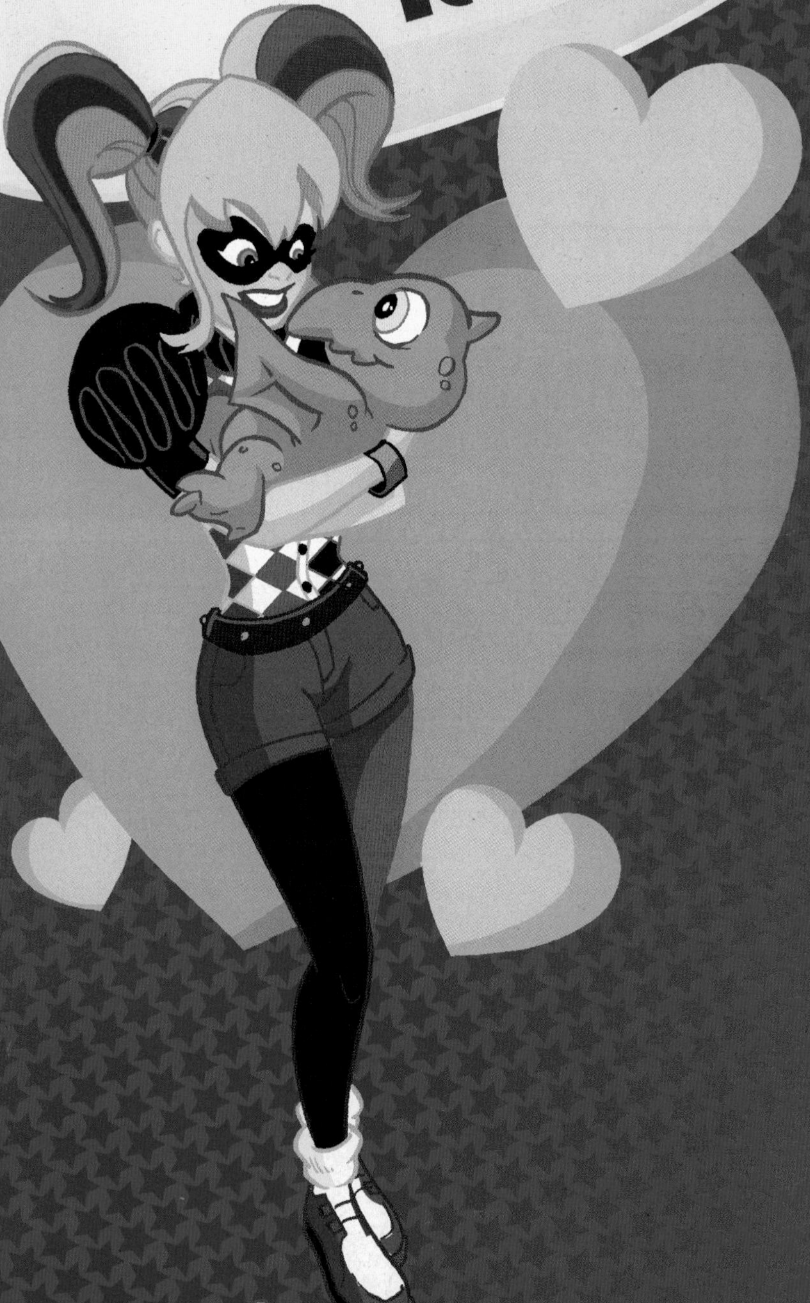

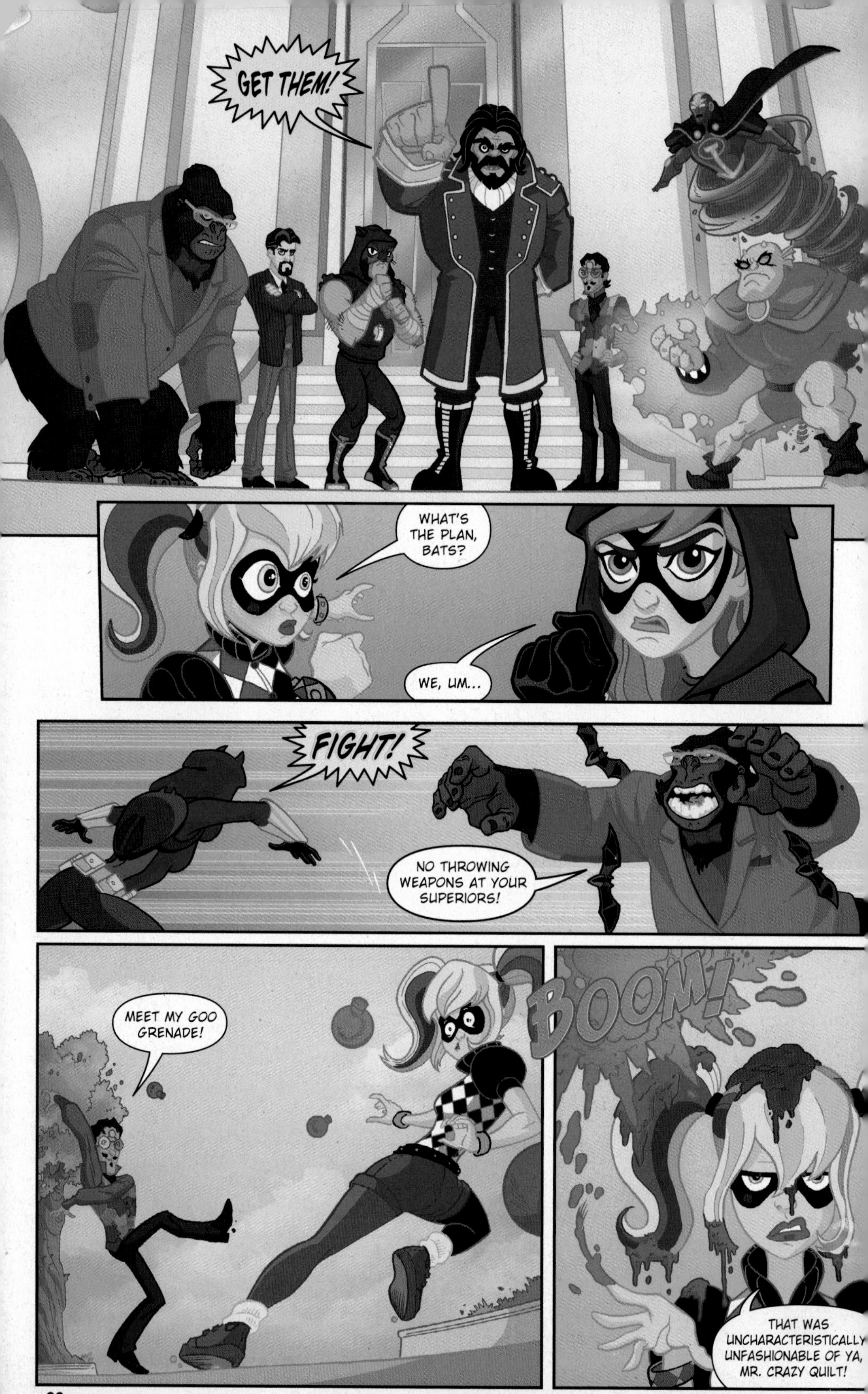
GET THEM!
WHAT'S THE PLAN, BATS?
WE, UM...
FIGHT!
NO THROWING WEAPONS AT YOUR SUPERIORS!
MEET MY GOO GRENADE!
BOOM!
THAT WAS UNCHARACTERISTICALLY UNFASHIONABLE OF YA, MR. CRAZY QUILT!

TIME TO TEACH THESE, UM, TEACHERS A LESSON!

THANKS A BAJILLION, WONDY!

HEY, RED TORNADO, GUESS WHO ACED HER FLYING TEST?

YOUR QUERY DOES NOT COMPUTE.

THIS IS FOR ALL THOSE TIMES YOU PUT ME IN DETENTION!

GRRRR!

I DARE YOU TO COME NEAR. YOUR SCREAMS I LONG TO HEAR.

WHOA! WATCH THE NAILS, PROFESSOR!

SLASH

KRASH

HURRY! GO GET THAT DINO EGG!

ON IT LIKE A SONNET!

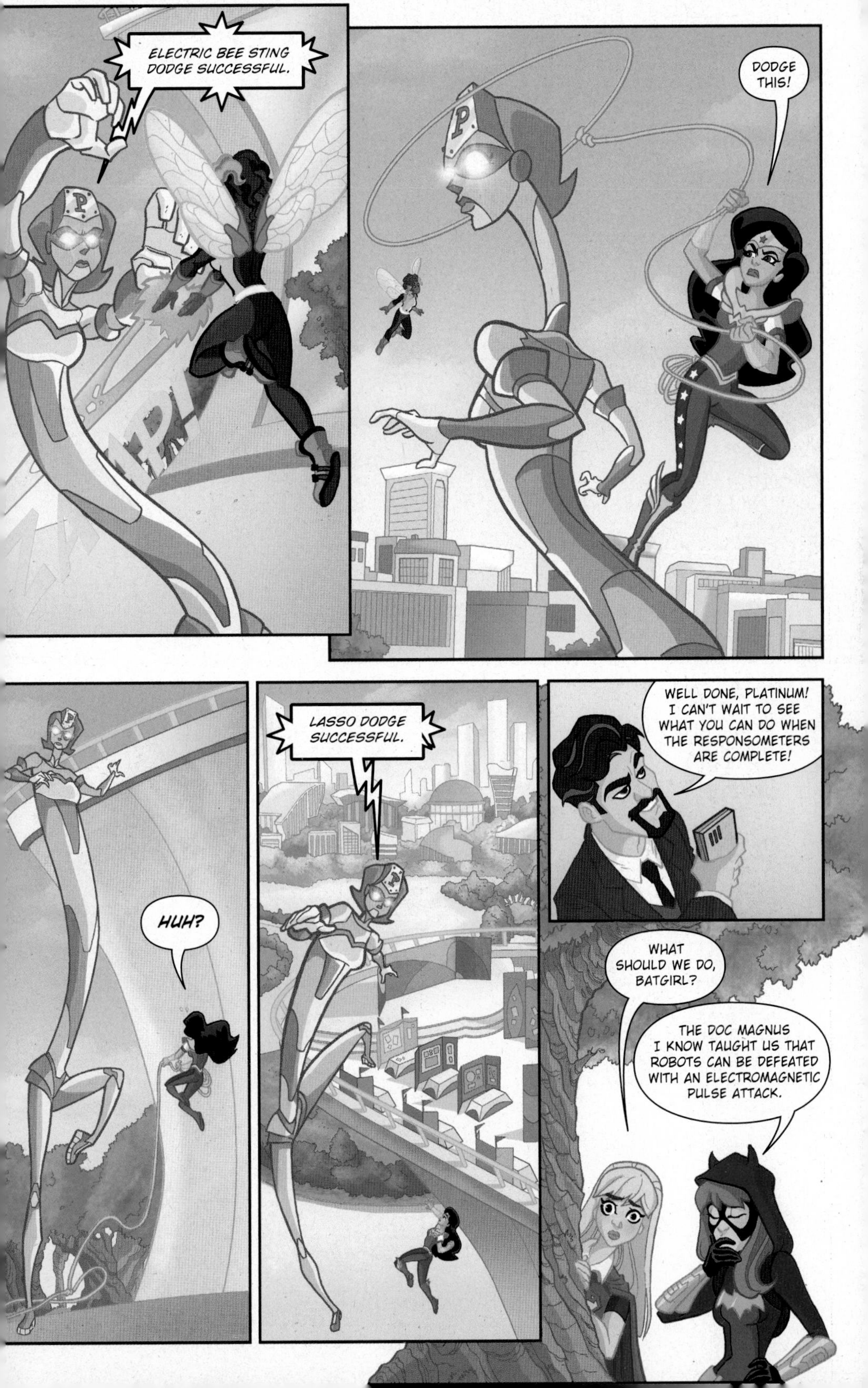
ELECTRIC BEE STING DODGE SUCCESSFUL.
DODGE THIS!
HUH?
LASSO DODGE SUCCESSFUL.
WELL DONE, PLATINUM! I CAN'T WAIT TO SEE WHAT YOU CAN DO WHEN THE RESPONSOMETERS ARE COMPLETE!
WHAT SHOULD WE DO, BATGIRL?
THE DOC MAGNUS I KNOW TAUGHT US THAT ROBOTS CAN BE DEFEATED WITH AN ELECTROMAGNETIC PULSE ATTACK.

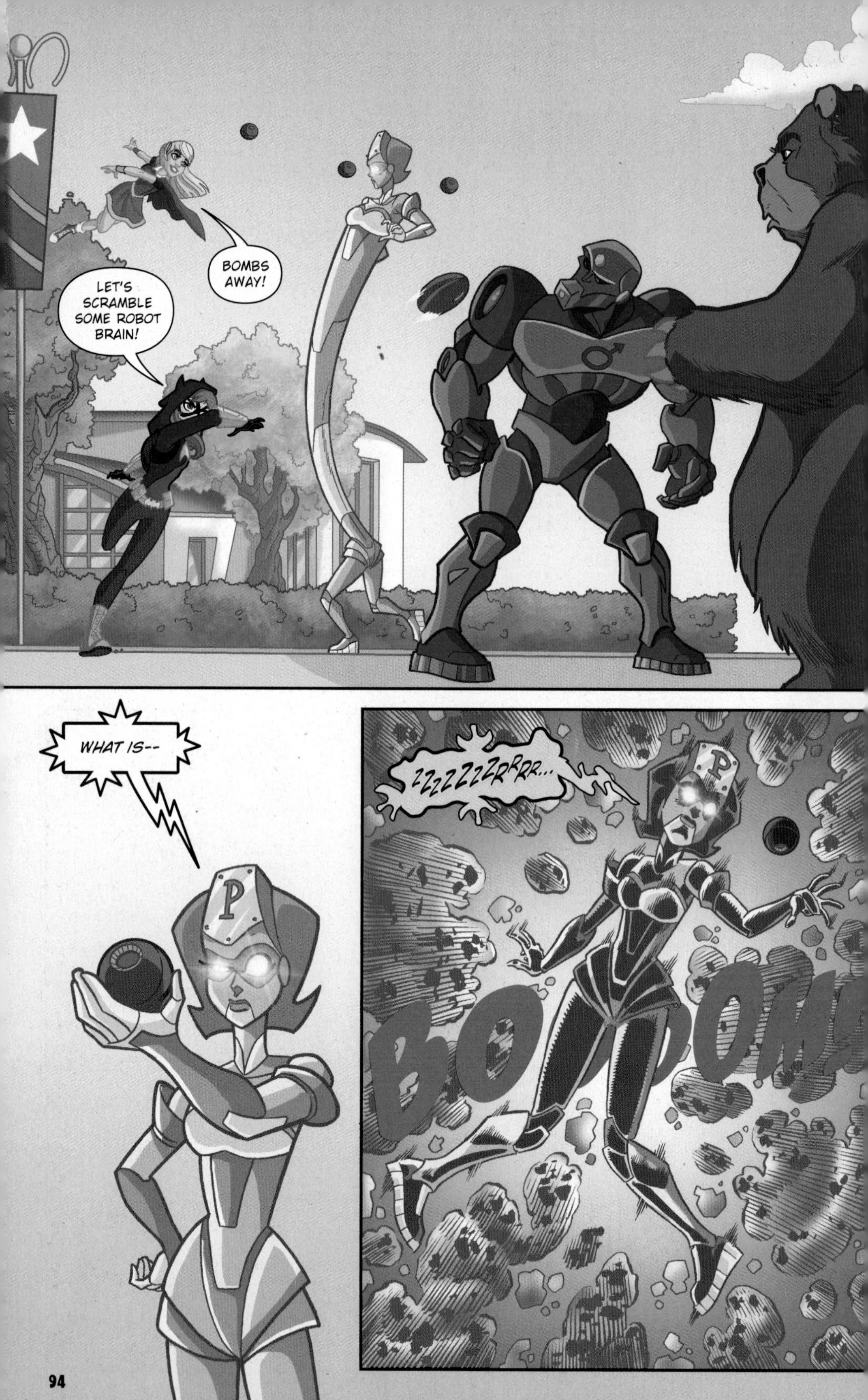
LET'S SCRAMBLE SOME ROBOT BRAIN!
BOMBS AWAY!
WHAT IS--
ZZZZZZZRRRR...
BOOM

-NGH!-

BECAUSE I WON'T LET THE FUTURE BE LIKE THAT!

OOF!

WHY HAVE YOU BEEN FOLLOWING ME?

IT'S OVER, LITTLE GIRL. YOU CAN'T CHANGE THE PAST, AND I WON'T GIVE YOU TH CHANCE TO CHANGE THE FUTURE.

YOU'VE SEEN THE FUTURE.

UM, I MEANT TO SAY--

YOU KNOW I WIN!

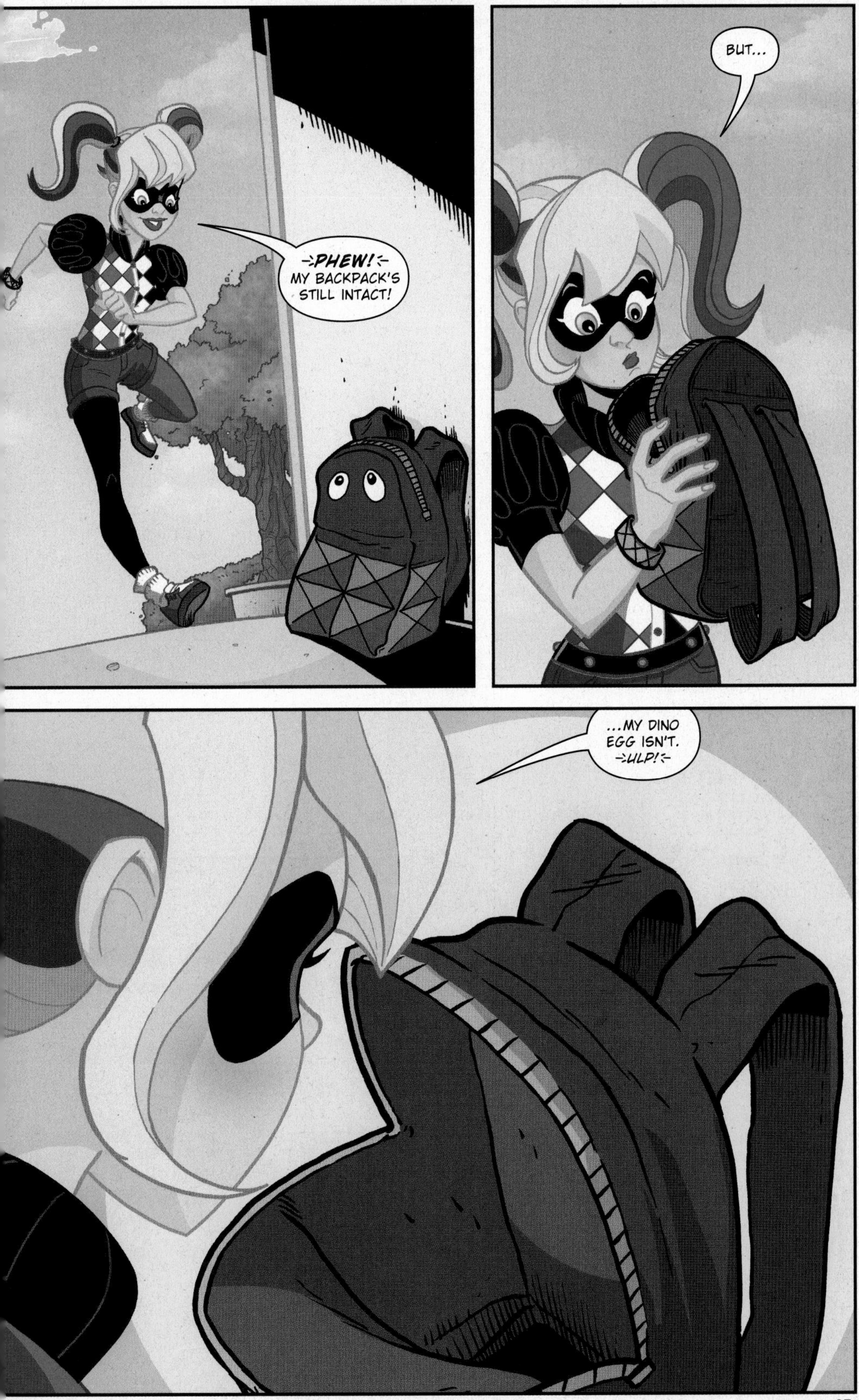

-PHEW!- MY BACKPACK'S STILL INTACT!
BUT...
...MY DINO EGG ISN'T. -ULP!-

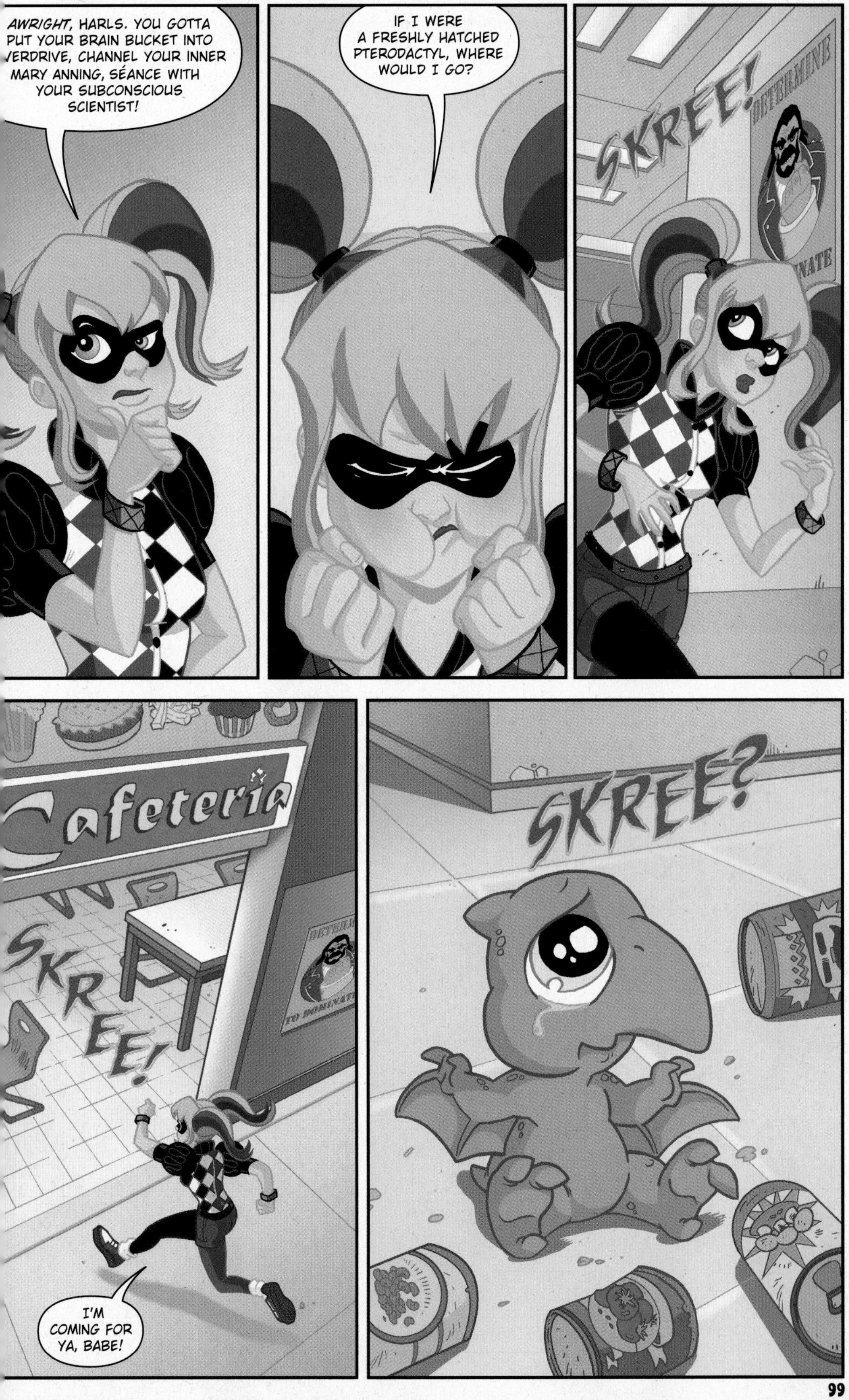
AWRIGHT, HARLS. YOU GOTTA PUT YOUR BRAIN BUCKET INTO VERDRIVE, CHANNEL YOUR INNER MARY ANNING, SÉANCE WITH YOUR SUBCONSCIOUS SCIENTIST!
IF I WERE A FRESHLY HATCHED PTERODACTYL, WHERE WOULD I GO?
SKREE!
DETERMINE
Cafeteria
SKREE!
TO DOMINATE
I'M COMING FOR YA, BABE!
SKREE?

SKREE?

YOU BELONG IN THE PAST AND I'M GOING TO MAKE SURE YOU GET THERE.

I WAS JUST TEASIN'. I'D CHANGE ALL THE DINO DIAPERS IN THE WORLD IF I COULD KEEP YA--BUT, OL' SMARTY-BATS IS RIGHT.

NO MATTER WHAT, I'M NOT GONNA RUIN THINGS THIS TIME.

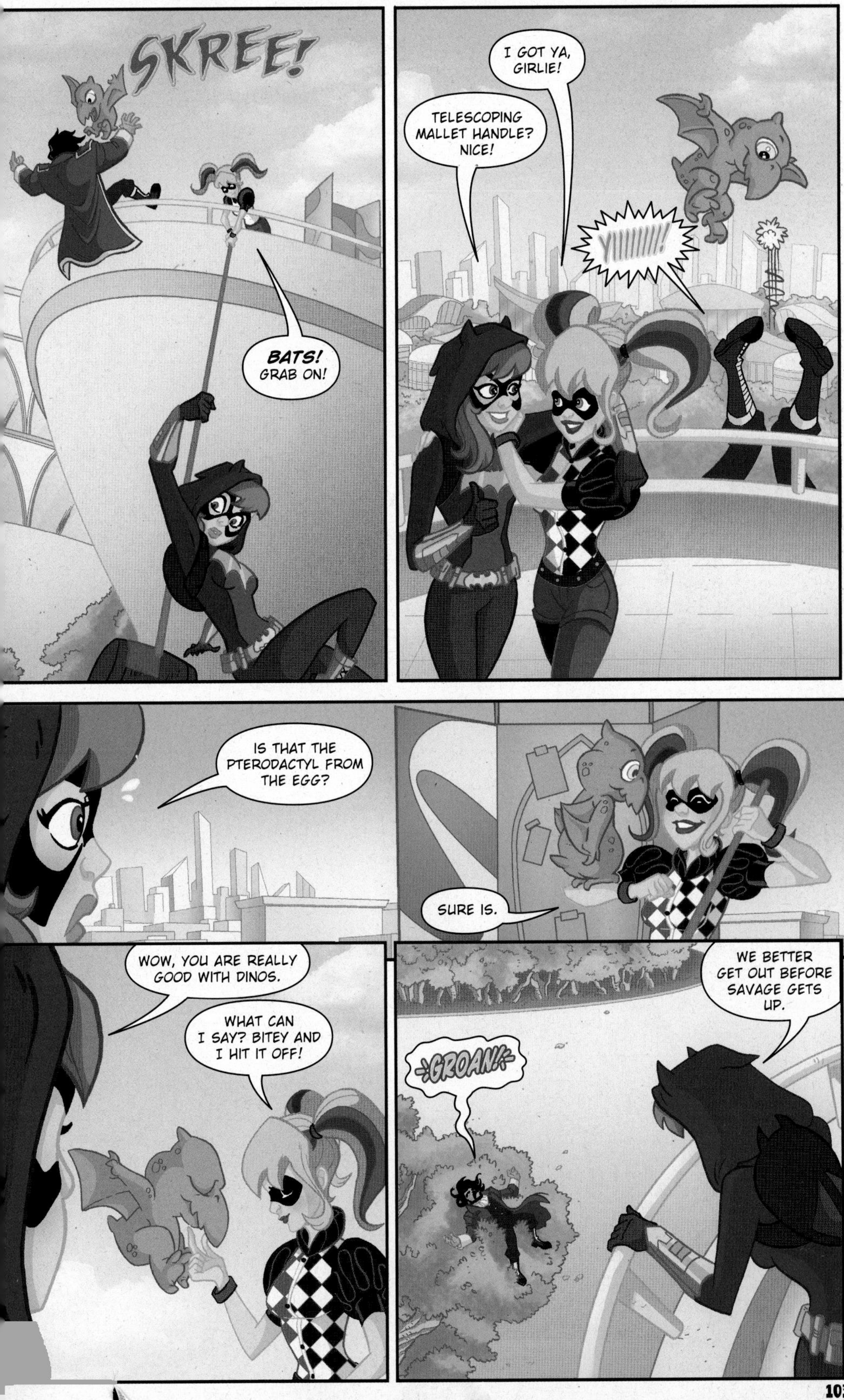
SKREE!
BATS! GRAB ON!
TELESCOPING MALLET HANDLE? NICE!
I GOT YA, GIRLIE!
YIIIIIIII!
IS THAT THE PTERODACTYL FROM THE EGG?
SURE IS.
WOW, YOU ARE REALLY GOOD WITH DINOS.
WHAT CAN I SAY? BITEY AND I HIT IT OFF!
GROAN!
WE BETTER GET OUT BEFORE SAVAGE GETS UP.

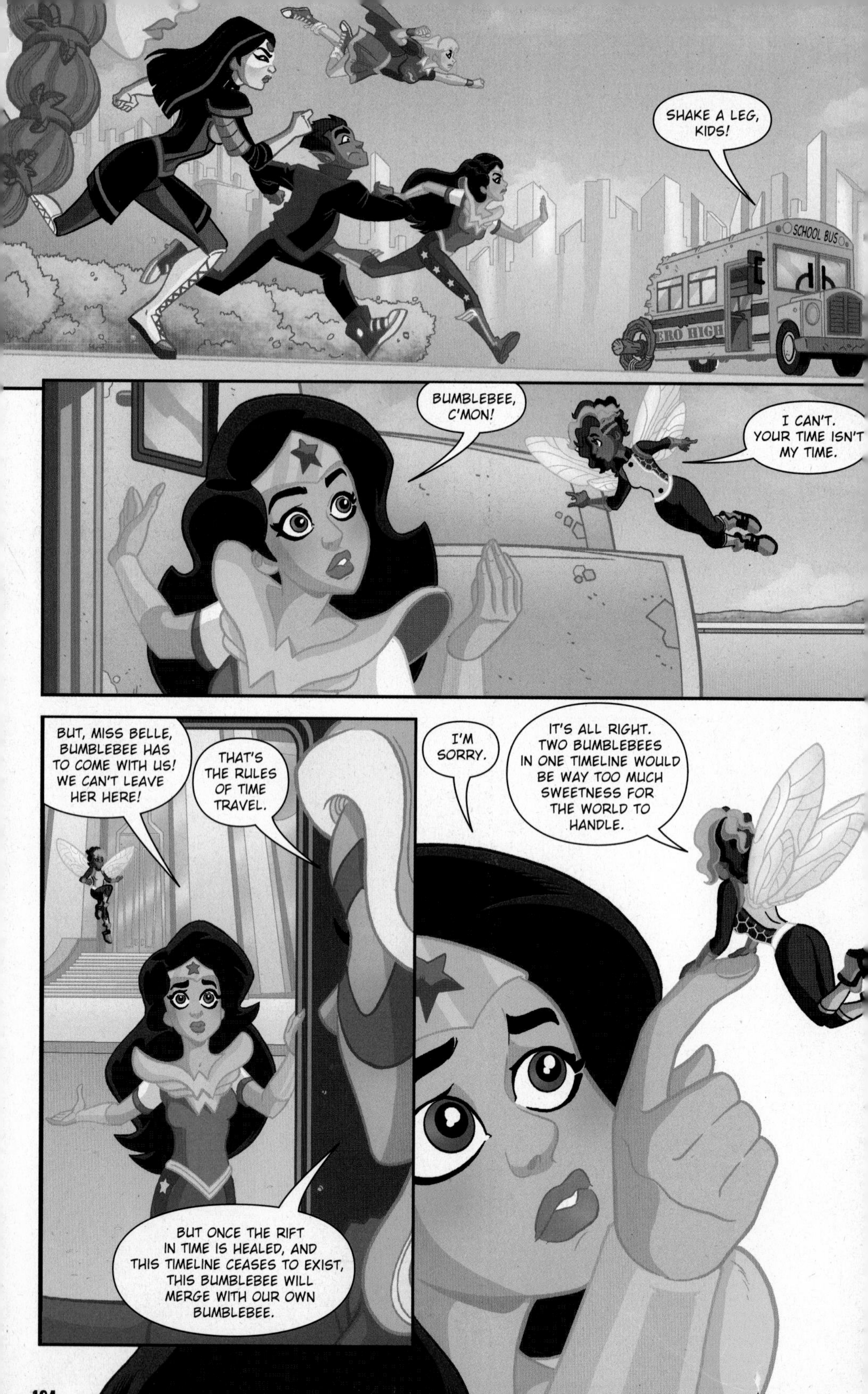
SHAKE A LEG, KIDS!
SCHOOL BUS
ERO HIGH
BUMBLEBEE, C'MON!
I CAN'T. YOUR TIME ISN'T MY TIME.
BUT, MISS BELLE, BUMBLEBEE HAS TO COME WITH US! WE CAN'T LEAVE HER HERE!
THAT'S THE RULES OF TIME TRAVEL.
I'M SORRY.
IT'S ALL RIGHT. TWO BUMBLEBEES IN ONE TIMELINE WOULD BE WAY TOO MUCH SWEETNESS FOR THE WORLD TO HANDLE.
BUT ONCE THE RIFT IN TIME IS HEALED, AND THIS TIMELINE CEASES TO EXIST, THIS BUMBLEBEE WILL MERGE WITH OUR OWN BUMBLEBEE.

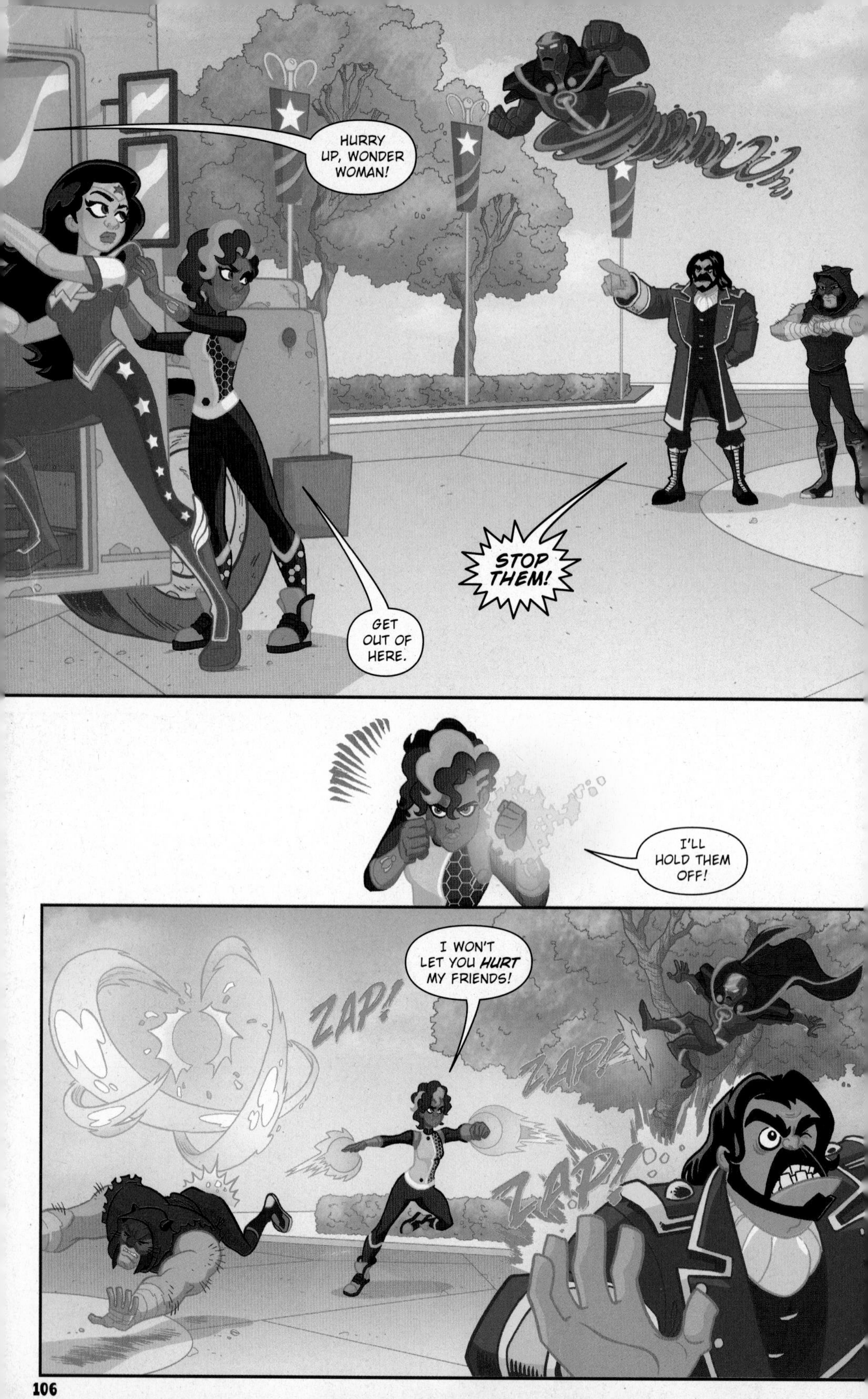
HURRY UP, WONDER WOMAN!
GET OUT OF HERE.
STOP THEM!
I'LL HOLD THEM OFF!
I WON'T LET YOU HURT MY FRIENDS!
ZAP!
ZAP!
ZAP!

AW, HE'S SO CUTE!

YEAH, NOT TO MENTION BRAVE, HEROIC, AND WITH A BITIN' SENSE OF HUMOR.

70,000 BC

70,000 BC

000 BC

00

000 BC

HERE WE ARE! BACK TO THE JURASSIC ERA!

YES! WE MADE IT!

PLUNK!

NOT TO RAIN ON Y'ALL'S PARADE, BUT IS ANYONE ELSE CONCERNED ABOUT THE FACT THAT WE'RE ABOUT TO FALL OVER THE EDGE OF A CLIFF?

SCHOOL BUS

RO HIGH

CHAPTER SIX
DÉJÀ VU

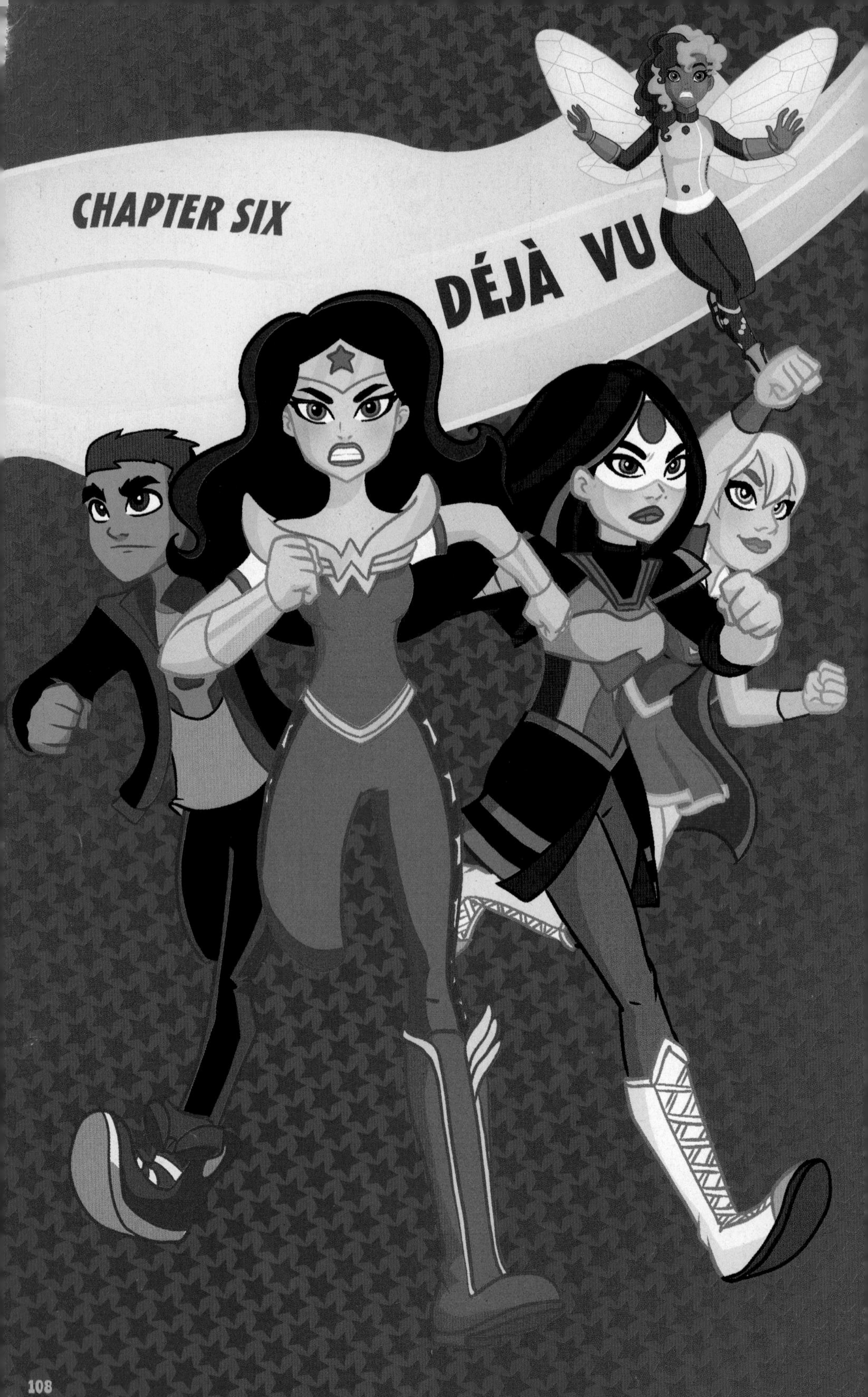

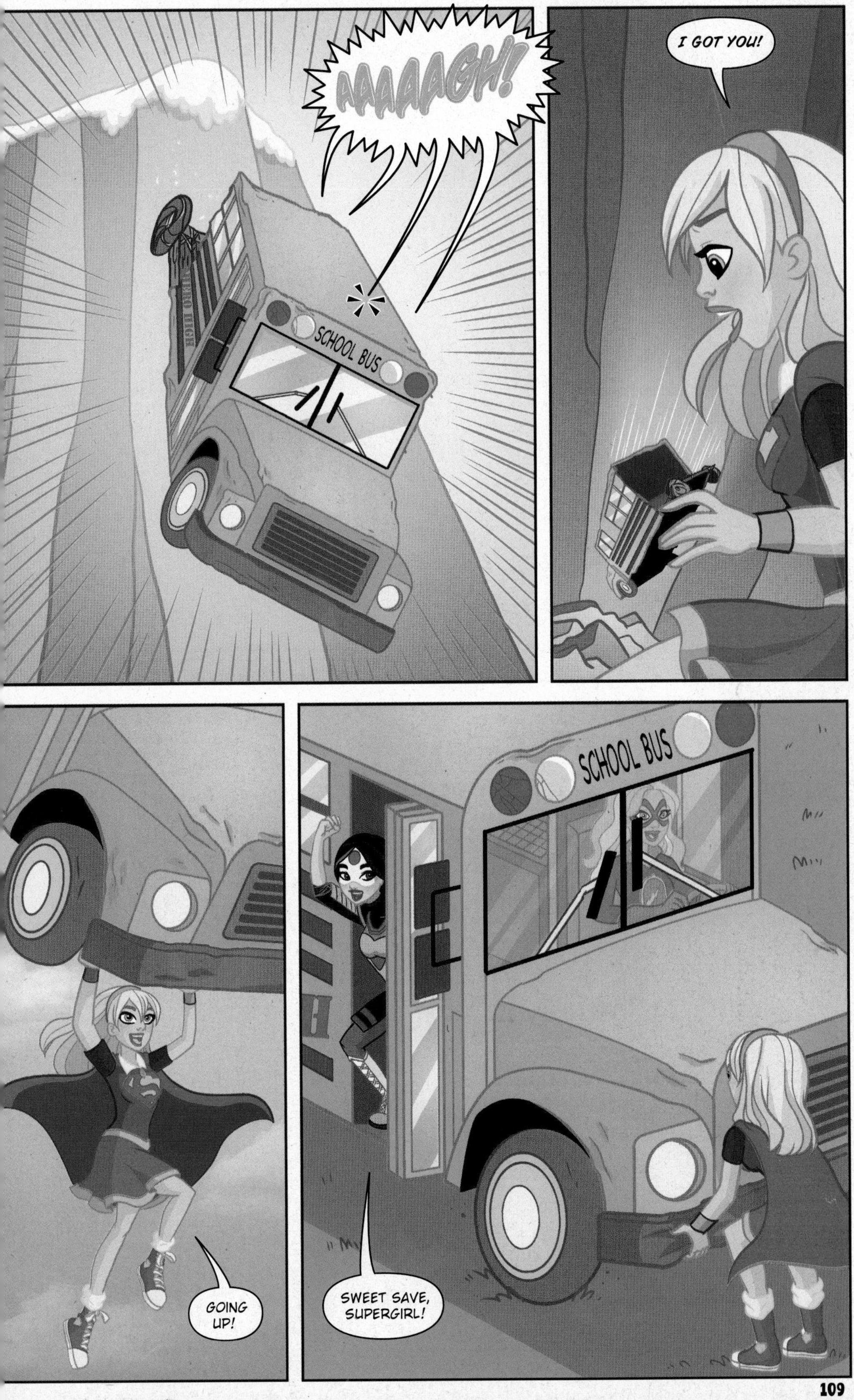
AAAAAAGH!
SCHOOL BUS
I GOT YOU!
SCHOOL BUS
GOING UP!
SWEET SAVE, SUPERGIRL!

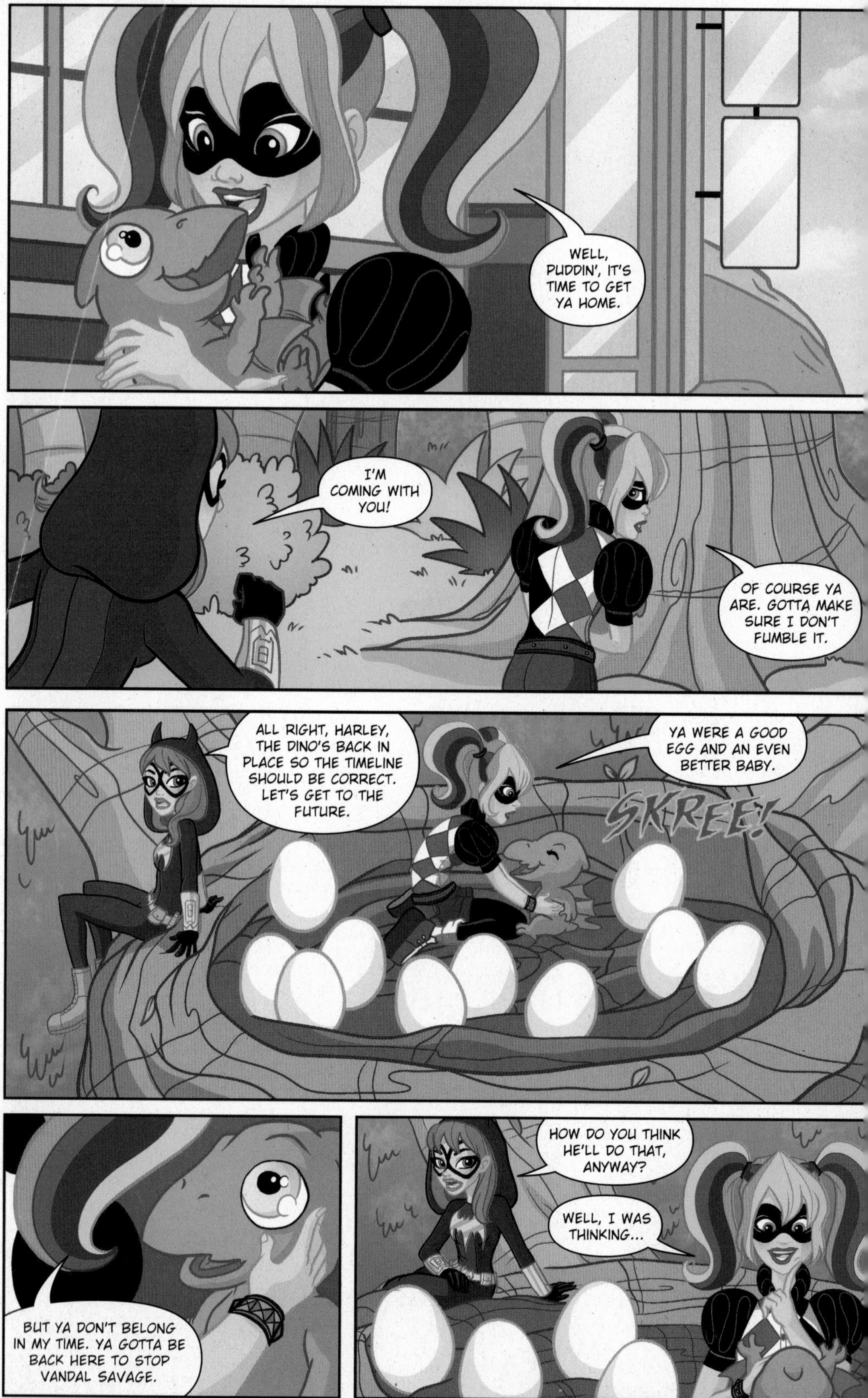
WELL, PUDDIN', IT'S TIME TO GET YA HOME.
I'M COMING WITH YOU!
OF COURSE YA ARE. GOTTA MAKE SURE I DON'T FUMBLE IT.
ALL RIGHT, HARLEY, THE DINO'S BACK IN PLACE SO THE TIMELINE SHOULD BE CORRECT. LET'S GET TO THE FUTURE.
YA WERE A GOOD EGG AND AN EVEN BETTER BABY.
SKREE!
BUT YA DON'T BELONG IN MY TIME. YA GOTTA BE BACK HERE TO STOP VANDAL SAVAGE.
HOW DO YOU THINK HE'LL DO THAT, ANYWAY?
WELL, I WAS THINKING...

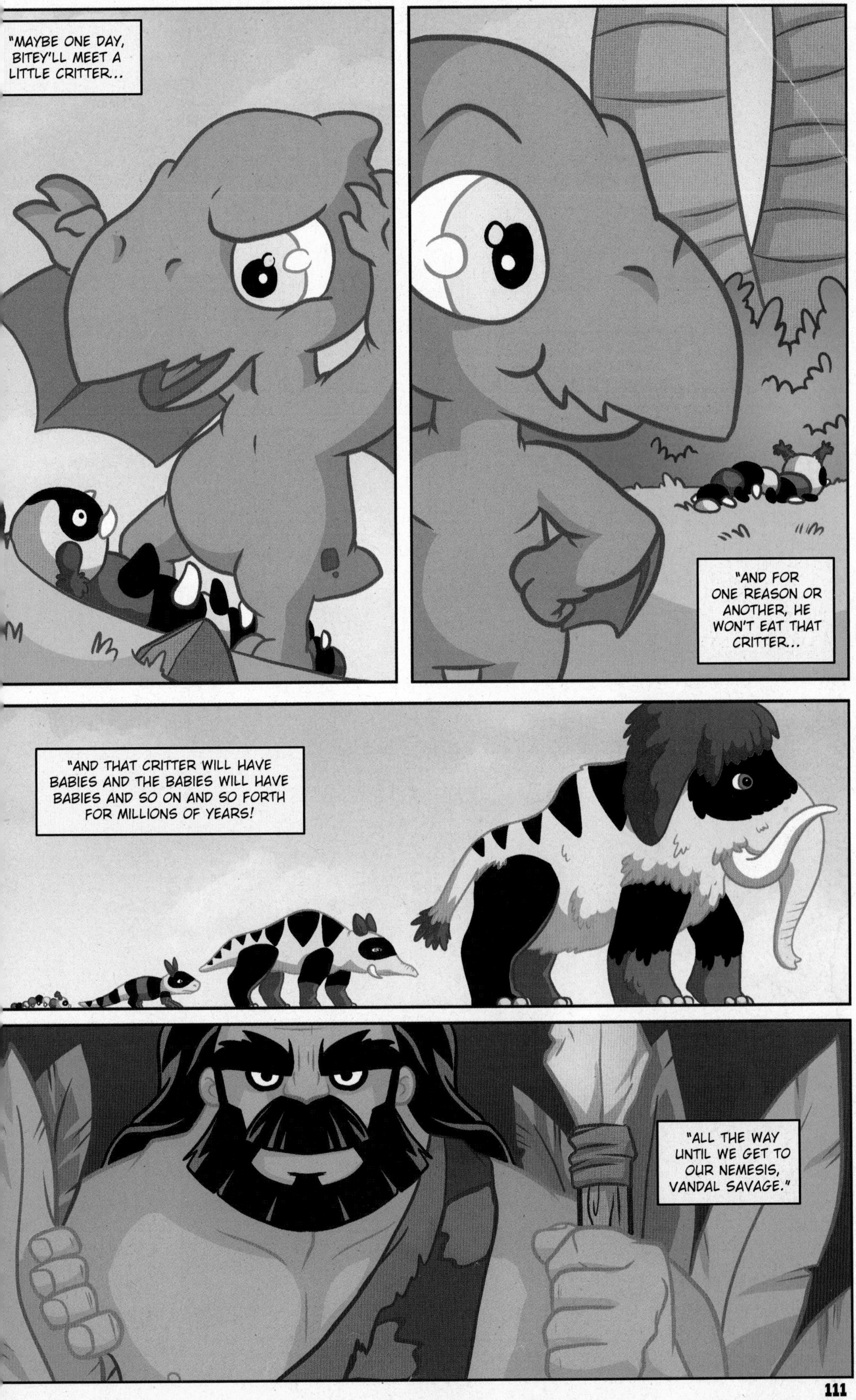
"MAYBE ONE DAY, BITEY'LL MEET A LITTLE CRITTER..
"AND FOR ONE REASON OR ANOTHER, HE WON'T EAT THAT CRITTER...
"AND THAT CRITTER WILL HAVE BABIES AND THE BABIES WILL HAVE BABIES AND SO ON AND SO FORTH FOR MILLIONS OF YEARS!
"ALL THE WAY UNTIL WE GET TO OUR NEMESIS, VANDAL SAVAGE."

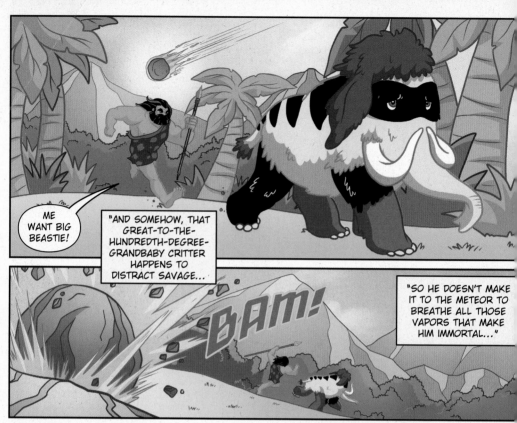

ME WANT BIG BEASTIE!

"AND SOMEHOW, THAT GREAT-TO-THE-HUNDREDTH-DEGREE-GRANDBABY CRITTER HAPPENS TO DISTRACT SAVAGE..."

BAM!

"SO HE DOESN'T MAKE IT TO THE METEOR TO BREATHE ALL THOSE VAPORS THAT MAKE HIM IMMORTAL..."

GRRRRRR!

EEEEE! ME SORRY!

"...AND WE CAN ALL LIVE HAPPILY EVER AFTER!"

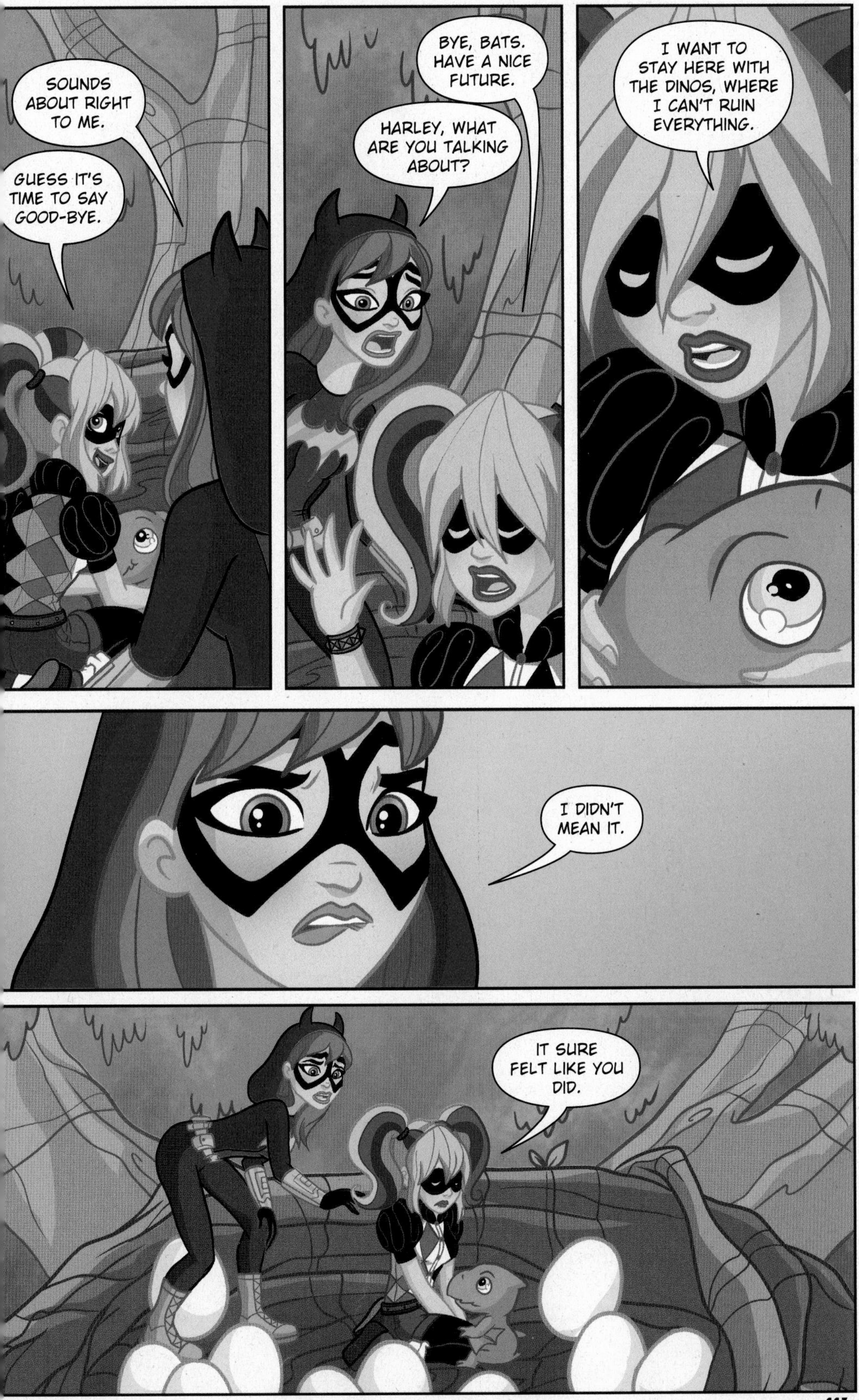
SOUNDS ABOUT RIGHT TO ME.
GUESS IT'S TIME TO SAY GOOD-BYE.
BYE, BATS. HAVE A NICE FUTURE.
HARLEY, WHAT ARE YOU TALKING ABOUT?
I WANT TO STAY HERE WITH THE DINOS, WHERE I CAN'T RUIN EVERYTHING.
I DIDN'T MEAN IT.
IT SURE FELT LIKE YOU DID.

I WAS JUST UPSET THAT YOU TOOK THE EGG.

WELL, I TOOK IT 'CUZ I WANTED TO BE THE BEST AT SOMETHIN'.

I KNOW I CAN'T OUT-FLY WONDY OR OUT-GROW IVY OR OUT-EYE-LASER SUPES.

BUT I THOUGHT I WAS PRETTY GOOD AT DINOS...UNTIL *YOU* CAME ALONG.

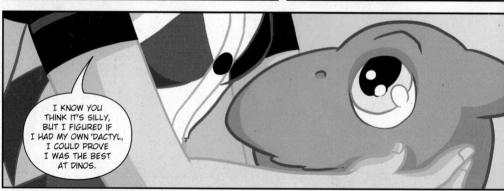

I KNOW YOU THINK IT'S SILLY, BUT I FIGURED IF I HAD MY OWN 'DACTYL, I COULD PROVE I WAS THE BEST AT DINOS.

I DON'T THINK IT'S SILLY. I GET IT--

HOW COULD YA? YOU'RE THE BEST AT VEHICLES, 'PUTERS, BUILDIN' BAT BUNKERS, AND SAVIN' THE DAY! AND I'M JUST FAIR-TO-MIDDLIN' HARLEY, *RUINING EVERYTHING.*

I'M SORRY. REALLY *SORRY.* IF I COULD GO BACK IN TIME AND TAKE BACK SAYING THAT, I WOULD.

BUT WE ALL KNOW HOW TERRIBLE I AM AT TIME TRAVEL.

HA! I GUESS WE DID FIND ONE THING YOU WEREN'T GREAT AT.

THINK YOU'RE GREAT AT LOTS OF THINGS, LIKE ACROBATICS AND MAKING PEOPLE LAUGH, AND STEALING DINO EGGS WITHOUT ME SUSPECTING--

YEAH, POINT HARLEY!

AND I THINK YOU *ARE* BETTER AT DINOS THAN ME.

AW, SHUCKS!

ZZZZZZZ

115

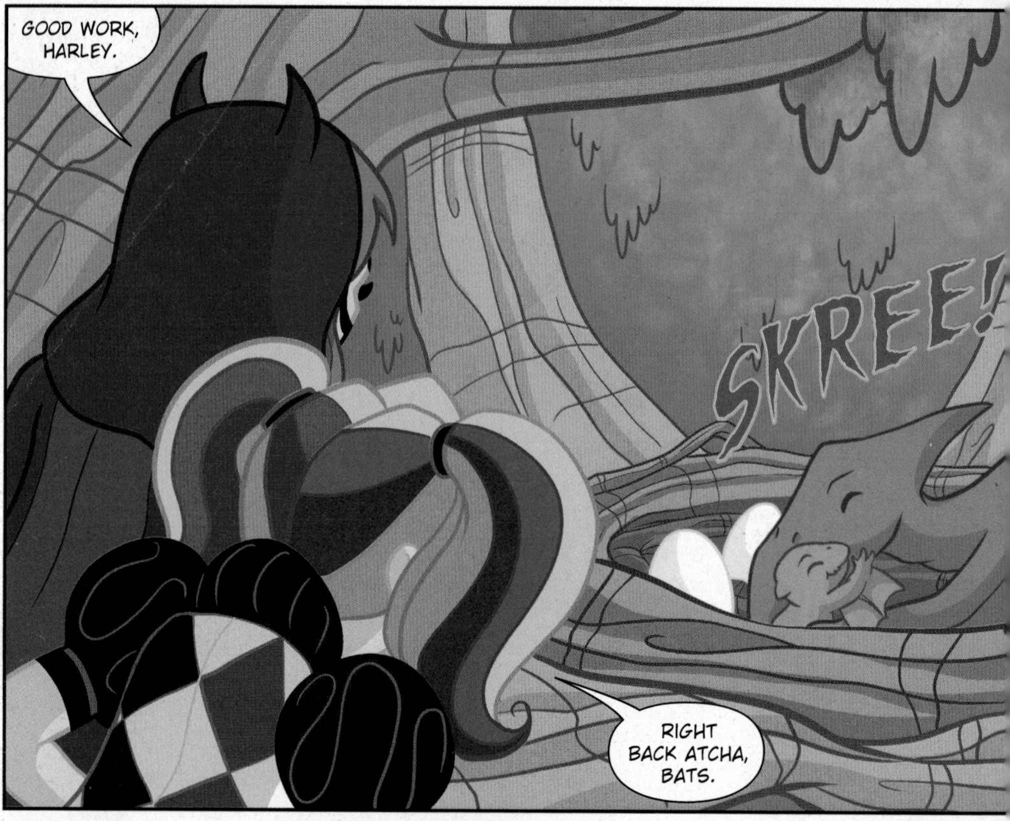
GOOD WORK, HARLEY.
SKREE!
RIGHT BACK ATCHA, BATS.

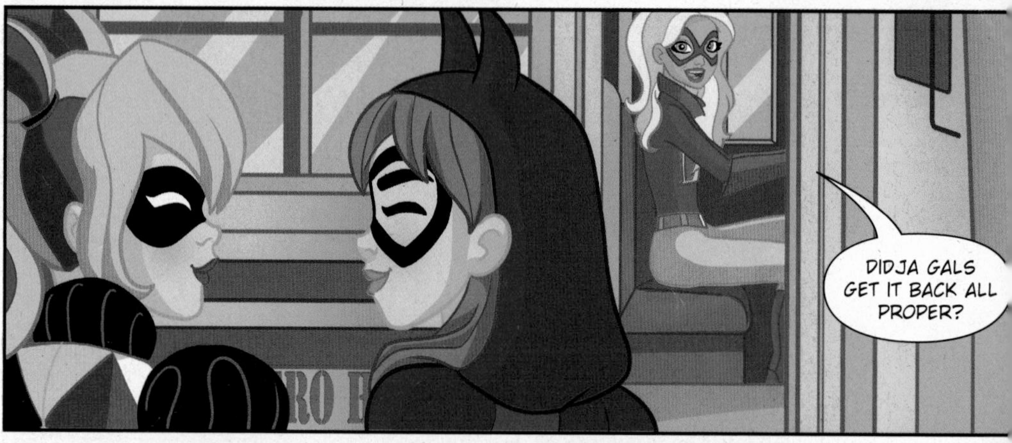
DIDJA GALS GET IT BACK ALL PROPER?

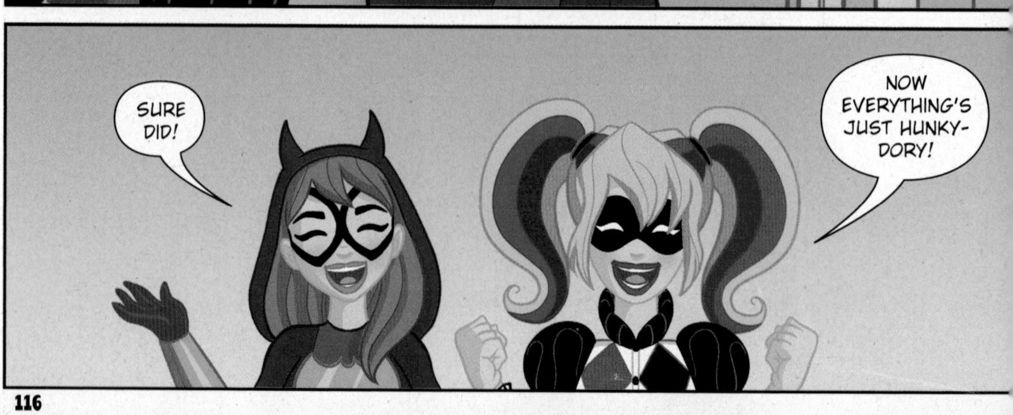
SURE DID!
NOW EVERYTHING'S JUST HUNKY-DORY!

HOME SWEET HOME!

PLUNK!

AW, SUCCULENT SUPER HERO HIGH VEGETATION!

BACK ALREADY? I HAVEN'T EVEN STARTED MY FIELD TRIP MAKEUP REPORT YET!

IT'S YOU! IT'S REALLY YOU!

YEAH, IT'S ME. WHO ELSE WOULD IT BE?

DAD! DO YOU KNOW WHO VANDAL SAVAGE IS?

VANDAL SAVAGE? CAN'T SAY I'M FAMILIAR WITH THE NAME. IS HE IN ONE OF THOSE BOY BANDS?

IF I KNEW NOT KNOWING THINGS GOT ME HUGS, I WOULD NOT KNOW MORE OFTEN! NOW I BETTER GO LET PRINCIPAL FOX KNOW YOU'VE SAFELY RETURNED.

THAT'S THE RIGHT ANSWER!

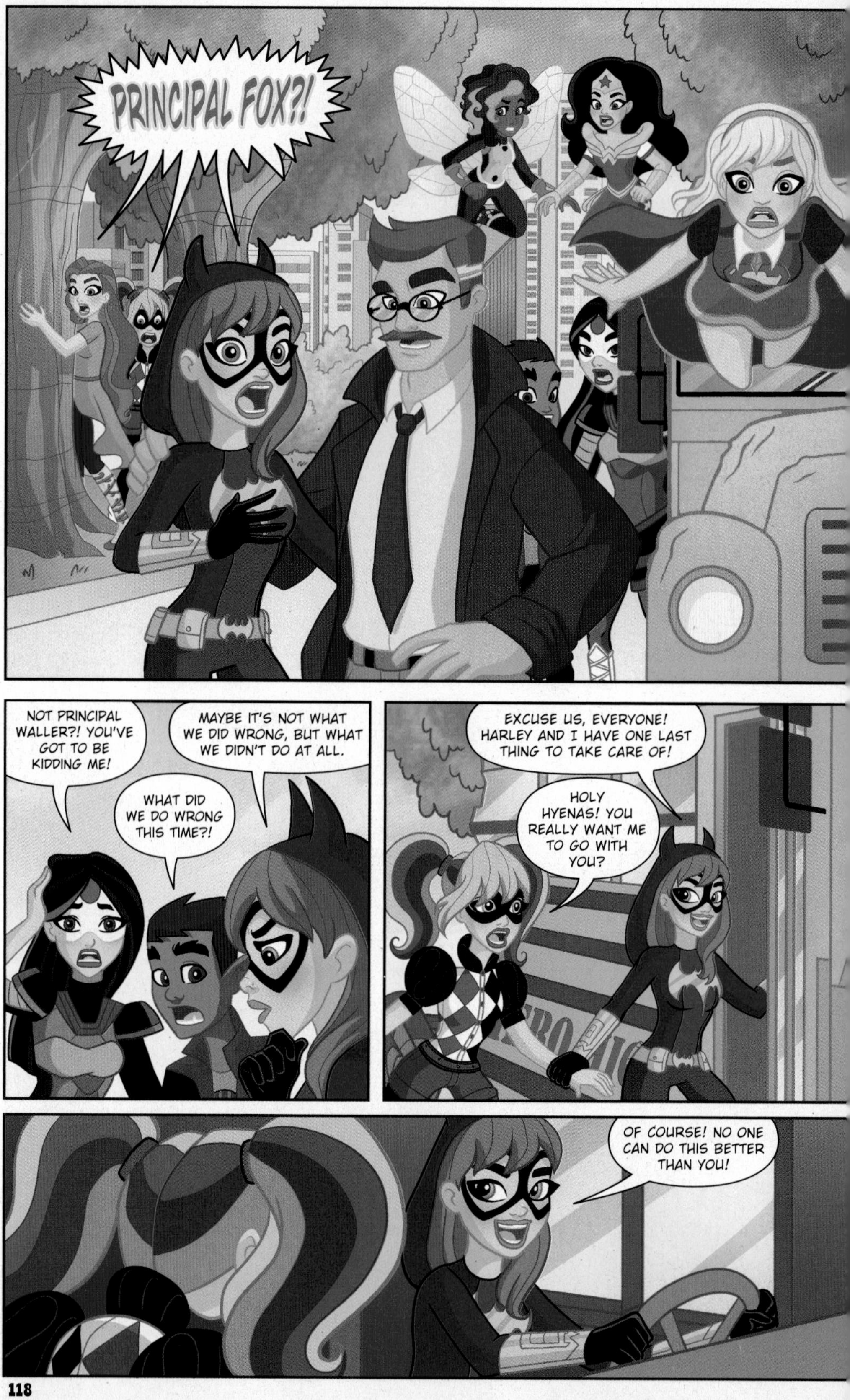

PRINCIPAL FOX?!
NOT PRINCIPAL WALLER?! YOU'VE GOT TO BE KIDDING ME!
WHAT DID WE DO WRONG THIS TIME?!
MAYBE IT'S NOT WHAT WE DID WRONG, BUT WHAT WE DIDN'T DO AT ALL.
EXCUSE US, EVERYONE! HARLEY AND I HAVE ONE LAST THING TO TAKE CARE OF!
HOLY HYENAS! YOU REALLY WANT ME TO GO WITH YOU?
OF COURSE! NO ONE CAN DO THIS BETTER THAN YOU!

1914.

HEY, AMELIA!

STILL FLYIN' THAT KITE, HUH?

NOT JUST FLYING A KITE--I'M STUDYING THE AERONAUTICAL MOVEMENT OF THE KITE IN SPACE.

Y'SEE, THERE'S SOMETHING ABOUT FLYING THAT SPEAKS TO ME.

YEAH, BABY!

POW! AVIATION PIONEERING ON!

PLUNK!

"A FOUR-LETTER WORD FOR SANDWICH..."

HMMM... HERO!

SOLOMON GRUNDY, BORN ON A MONDAY--

:-AAGH!-:
MONSTER!

WE GOT A GRUMBLIN' GRUNDY THAT NEEDS TAKIN' DOWN A NOTCH!

POW! HERO ON!

REAL-LIFE SUPER HEROES? RAD!

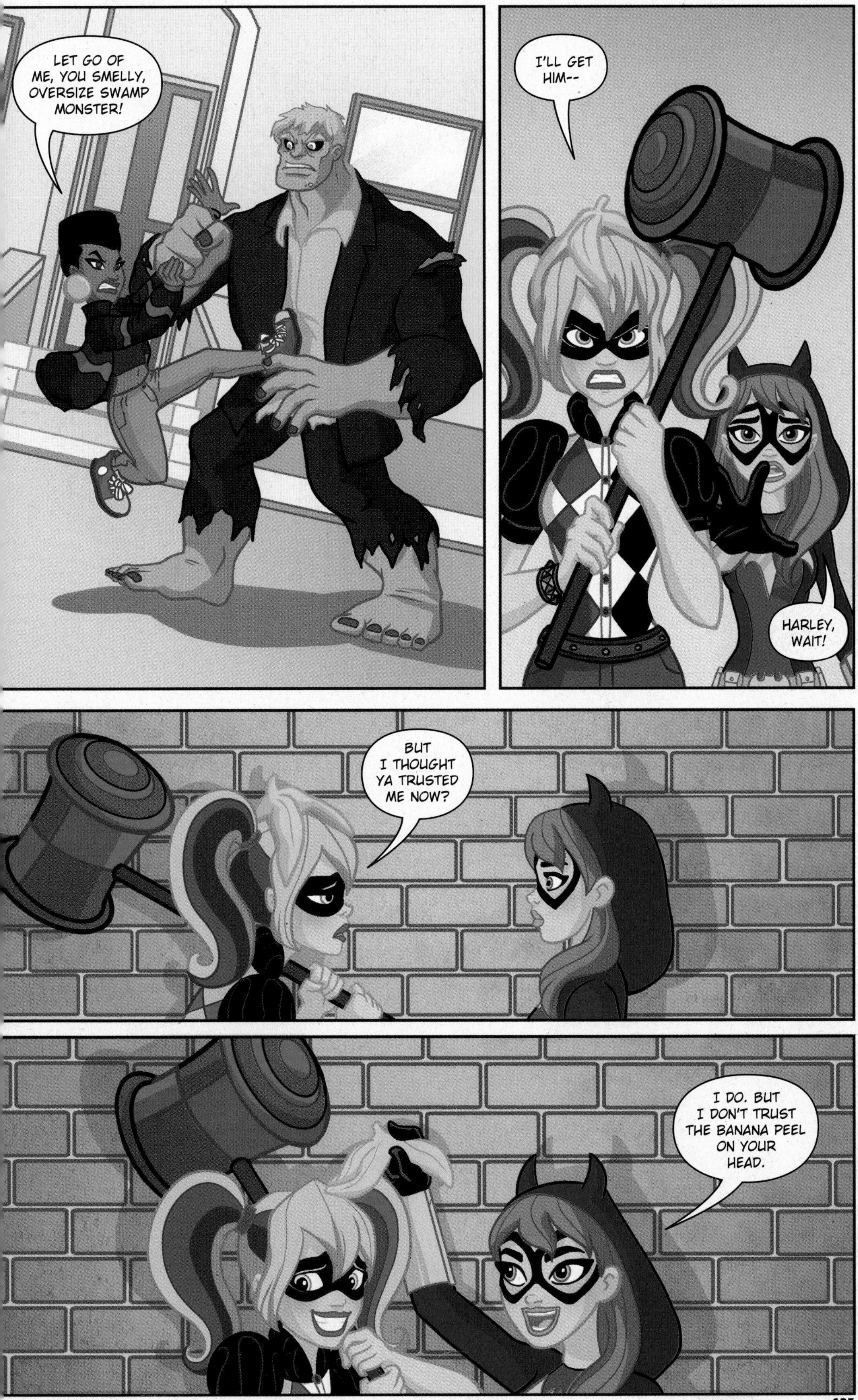
LET GO OF ME, YOU SMELLY, OVERSIZE SWAMP MONSTER!
I'LL GET HIM--
HARLEY, WAIT!
BUT I THOUGHT YA TRUSTED ME NOW?
I DO. BUT I DON'T TRUST THE BANANA PEEL ON YOUR HEAD.

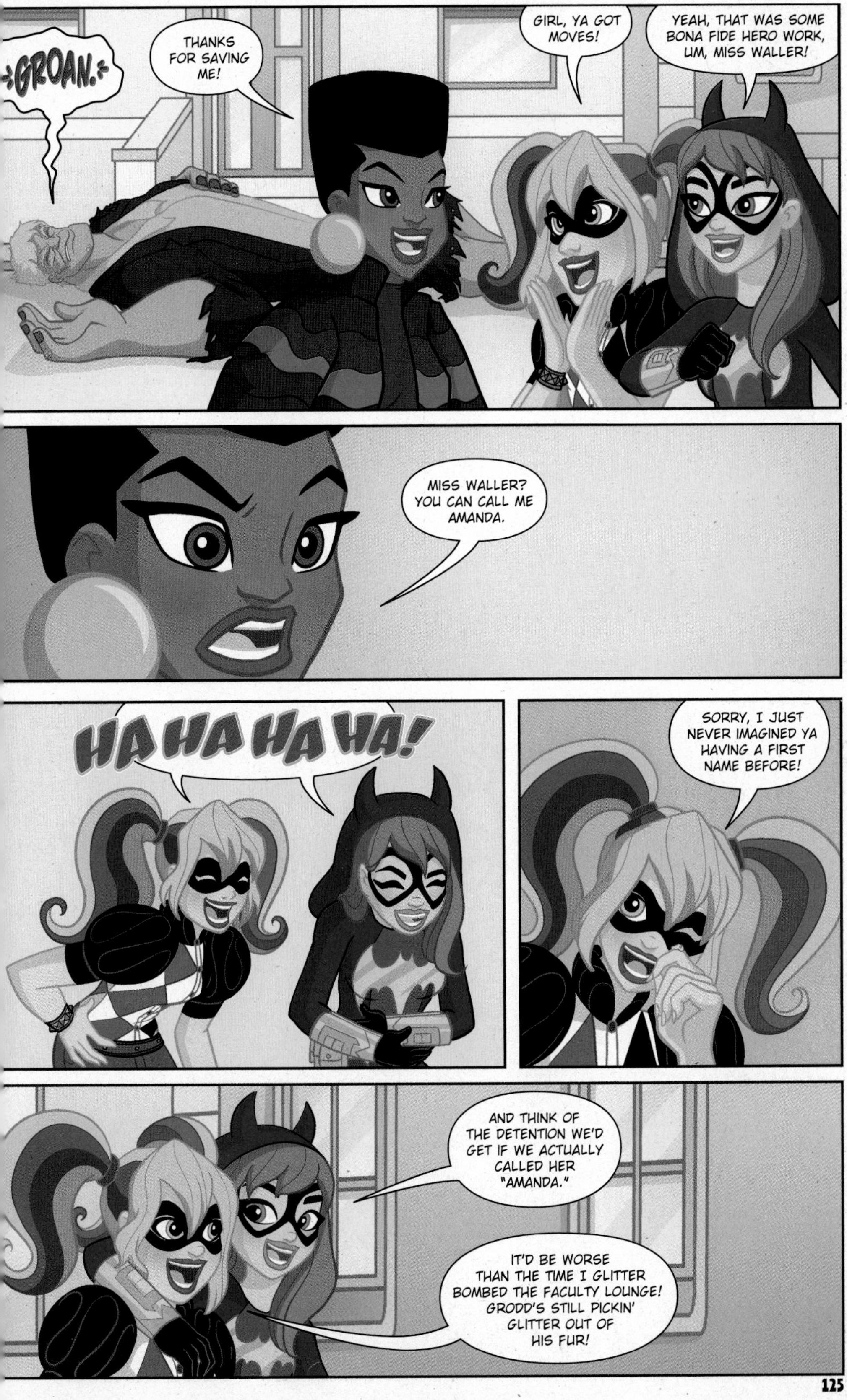
GROAN.
THANKS FOR SAVING ME!
GIRL, YA GOT MOVES!
YEAH, THAT WAS SOME BONA FIDE HERO WORK, UM, MISS WALLER!
MISS WALLER? YOU CAN CALL ME AMANDA.
HA HA HA HA HA!
SORRY, I JUST NEVER IMAGINED YA HAVING A FIRST NAME BEFORE!
AND THINK OF THE DETENTION WE'D GET IF WE ACTUALLY CALLED HER "AMANDA."
IT'D BE WORSE THAN THE TIME I GLITTER BOMBED THE FACULTY LOUNGE! GRODD'S STILL PICKIN' GLITTER OUT OF HIS FUR!

RRRRRRRRINNNGGGG!

AY TO O, BRO!

AND THEN I BECAME KING OF THE DINOSAURS!

YOU EXPERIENCED MUCH AMAZINGNESS ON THE TRIP OF FIELDING.

I'M NEVER TIME TRAVELING AGAIN!

NEXT TIME STAY HERE WITH ME!

THAT'S SO COOL! I CAN'T WAIT UNTIL I TAKE MISS BELLE'S CLASS!

WHERE WERE YOU GUYS? YOU MISSED THE TIME TRAVEL POP QUIZ!

WE WERE JUST, UM--

--HELPING THE WALL WITH A SPECIAL ASSIGNMENT!

IVY, CAREFUL WITH THAT PLANT NOW. I BEST NOT SEE IT ON THE NEWS TOMORROW.

OF COURSE--

PRINCIPAL WALLER!